IF WISHES
WERE HORSES

IF WISHES WERE HORSES

Jean Slaughter Doty

Macmillan Publishing Company
New York

c.1

J
Doty

Macmillan Publishing Company
866 Third Avenue, New York, N.Y. 10022
Collier Macmillan Canada, Inc.

Printed in the United States of America

10   9   8   7   6   5   4   3   2   1

Library of Congress Cataloging in Publication Data
Doty, Jean Slaughter, date.
    If wishes were horses.

    Summary: Thirteen-year-old Stephany and her older
sister Cam struggle to keep their horse farm going after
their father's death.
    [1. Horses—Breeding—Fiction]   I. Title.
PZ7.D7378If   1984   [Fic]   84-882
ISBN 0-02-733020-6

4/26/85
B+T
10.95

To all of us who dream of the foals of tomorrow

CHAPTER
One

I never could understand why a telephone ringing in the
night, in the dark, always sounded like a scream.

When the phone rang on the desk in the stable office
at three o'clock in the morning, I grabbed for it in the
darkness. But I'd forgotten I'd wrapped myself in two soft
stable blankets before I'd fallen asleep in the chair.

The two cats snuggled on top of me didn't help much,
either. It seemed forever before I was able to untangle
one arm to snatch at the shrieking phone.

1

"Hello." My voice came out in a croak.

"Stephany? Is that you, Steph?"

"It's me," I said, pulling my other arm out of the folds of the blankets and fumbling for the desk light. "Jimmy." I recognized his voice—Jimmy Conner, whose family had raised enormous white cattle on the farm next to ours, just across the wide shallow river that divided the land.

Jimmy had always liked our horses a lot more than his family's beef cattle, and he'd spent most of his waking hours with us at our Thunder Rock Farm. He'd watched and worked with my father any way he could, along with the trainers and managers who ran the broodmare stable, helping in the breaking of our young Thoroughbreds and their preliminary training before they were sold or sent off to the races. He'd practically grown up with my older sister Camilla and me. Jimmy was a racehorse trainer on his own now. His parents had retired to Arizona. The farm next to Thunder Rock was his and the cattle were gone; there were horses in the pastures instead, and Jimmy was beginning to make a name for himself as a trainer with a small number of winning young horses.

"I need to speak to Camilla," Jimmy said. "It's important."

"At three o'clock in the morning, I should hope it's important," I said a little sharply. I found the light and turned it on and gave the clock on the desk a thump to make sure the alarm didn't go off, which it was about to do. "Anyway, it doesn't matter, because Camilla's not here."

Jimmy's voice raised a notch or two. "What do you mean, she's not there? Where is she?"

"She went to a dance at the country club. With Cliff. Cliff Bennett. She should be back soon, though."

"I thought Cliff was away," Jimmy said. There was a pause. "Never mind. Your sister should have more sense. But I can't get into this right now. Steph, you're in charge over there, I guess—"

"You bet I am, with three mares due to foal," I said. "I'm stable manager and night watchperson—" I gave a deep, shuddering yawn.

"Then you'll have to help me. I need a horse. Right away."

I sighed. "Jimmy, you know we've got all kinds of horses. What particular horse have you got in mind? What kind of horse is a three-o'clock-in-the-morning horse?"

"The mare. The tall gray one with the ears."

Even at that awful hour, I had to laugh. I recognized the description. It was perfect. "Rosie," I said. Rosie was a Thoroughbred. Her registered name was Roses Red and she'd been born right here on Thunder Rock Farm out of one of our best mares. She was bred to be a racehorse,

3

but she grew too big too fast. When all the other yearlings were light and quick on their feet, Rosie was all angles and bones and awkward strides, and wore her long ears at funny angles—it could only be Rosie Jimmy meant.

Cam and I thought Rosie was marvelous, just for us. When Rosie was barely three years old, she'd let us climb on her back in her stall or out in the pasture. We thumped her sides with our bare heels and she never minded at all—not like the swifter little racehorses who were like swallows in the air and ready to dip and swing at the fall of a leaf, full of life and joy, but not much fun for youngsters to ride. In fact, we were forbidden to go near them. And once we outgrew the first fat little Shetlands Dad had given us, Rosie was always at Thunder Rock for us to ride and share.

By the time she was six years old, Rosie was a cloudy gray with a white mane and tail. She'd stopped growing, filled out, and become a tall, strong mare with a powerful way of going that made some of Dad's friends speak wistfully of the Maryland Hunt Cup and the English Grand National.

"Bred to the purple," Dad would say sternly every spring. "This mare's too good to be a toy for you two kids."

Then he'd laugh at our anxious expressions and give us a hug. "She'll produce some fine foals for us one day, but there's no hurry. Have fun."

And we did have fun with Rosie. I closed my eyes as I thought sleepily of Rosie and all the happy rides we'd shared all through the good times. It seemed so long ago. Galloping cross-country, jumping every fence we could find. Taking her swimming in the river on silvery summer afternoons. Cam and I riding her together to picnics under the willows near the river, or deeper in the woods, where the huge boulder stood with a streak of jagged gray on one side—the mark looked like a pattern of lightning engraved on the stone, and gave Thunder Rock its name. Sometimes we'd ride out with the young racehorses, Rosie in the lead and the spooky little yearlings following her with their exercise riders. The young horses would learn by watching her not to be afraid of birds and cloud shadows—perfectly ordinary things they'd seen every day in their pastures, but which would mysteriously become monsters and invaders from outer space when they were first ridden out under saddle. . . . My mind wandered dreamily.

"Stephany?" said Jimmy. "Have you gone back to sleep?"

"Nope." I blinked and rubbed my tired eyes.

"I need to borrow your mare tonight. I must pick her up tonight, or it'll be too late."

I yawned again. There wasn't much use asking Jimmy why he needed Rosie in the middle of the night—it was obvious he had a reason important to him, and asking questions would get me nowhere. Not that the why of

5

it mattered. There was probably nobody else in the world I'd have trusted with Rosie, but if Jimmy needed her, it was okay.

"I'll get her ready," I said.

"I'll be right over with the van," Jimmy said quickly, sounding as though he was afraid I'd change my mind. "Will you meet me at the stables?"

"I'm already there," I said. "Here. Whatever. I'm in the stable office right now. I told you, we've got three mares due to foal. It's easier to stay here in the office than go back up to the house in between the times I've got to check the mares."

"Right. See you in about half an hour." No good-by, just the click of the disconnection followed by the bored hum in the phone. I put the phone back together and unwound myself from the folds of the thick blue and white plaid blankets.

The cats curled up again on the tangled heap of blankets and went back to sleep. I switched on the outside floodlights for Jimmy and the lights in the main aisle of the stable for me.

It was a damp, cold night. I could hear raindrops dribbling down the windows. I pulled on my jacket and tried not to worry about Cam, out somewhere in the rainy dark on the slippery back roads. Cliff always drove too fast in his zippy cars. I could picture him trying to impress

Cam, whizzing along the winding country roads that were never planned for his kind of driving, but for horses and ox carts and hay wagons and such.

I walked slowly down the stable aisle, looking into each stall as I went by.

All the horses were sacked out in their deep straw beds. Some of them opened their eyes and blinked at me as I stopped by their stalls, and the three broodmares nearly ready to foal changed positions uncomfortably, but they didn't get up. They were used to me or Cam looking in on them all through these last weary nights. I stopped a while by each of their stalls, but everything seemed quiet. There were no beginning signs of labor.

My own personal definition of eternity, I decided, was waiting for a mare to have her foal. The eleven months it took for a foal to be ready to be born didn't seem any time at all compared to the waiting and watching that filled the last few days and nights.

I turned my watch to the light. I couldn't believe Cam was so late. Something *must* have happened—

Not that I blamed Cliff for trying to keep her with him as long as he could. Camilla was special. She looked like a china doll, with pale silver-gold hair and blue-violet eyes. A doll to be put on a high shelf to be admired by anyone who saw her. She seemed as fragile as a magnolia or a gardenia blossom, and just as pretty. But she

7

could muck out a stall with the best of the hired help, which she was always willing to do, even during the good times when we'd actually had good help on the farm. She could handle a stallion or break a frightened yearling or help with the birth of a foal just about as well as anyone I knew.

She wouldn't forget I was watching over the three mares now, by myself, no matter how good a time she was having at the dance with Cliff. It must be nice for her, though, to be in a pretty room full of lights and music, with someone as handsome as Cliff beside her. They made a perfect couple. Everybody said so, and everybody kept telling me so, from the owner of the feed-and-grain store each time he made a delivery at the stable, to the ladies who used to stop by with their chatter and casseroles for Cam and me just after Dad died.

They hadn't come for long, because Cam and I were always busy with the horses or the land, straightening a sagging board of a fence or catching a merry pair of yearlings in a forty-acre pasture—not an easy thing to do. We never meant to be rude, but there was always so much work to be done by just the two of us on a place as big as ours that we didn't have time to be social.

CHAPTER
Two

I stopped to look carefully at the pretty red-gold chestnut mare, a daughter of the breathtaking Secretariat. She was waiting patiently in her soft bed of straw for the arrival of her first foal. Part of my mind studied the mare, and another part dipped and swung with crazy ideas. Maybe Cam had gone off with Cliff to be married—but I knew at the same time that this simply couldn't be true. Cam would have told me, and if she did decide to marry

Cliff, theirs would be a super-huge wedding. Cliff's family would insist on it. It would be the social bash of the whole state with retired senators, and governors from practically back to the time of the Civil War, a few ex-presidents, and almost anybody with a name anyone ever heard of among the guests.

But most important of all, I knew it wasn't like Cam to leave a thirteen-year-old in charge alone for more than a handful of hours at a time when mares were due to foal.

I left the chestnut mare and stopped at the next stall where a bigger mare, the color of dark melted chocolate, was dozing with her eyes half-shut. She opened them and turned her head toward me but didn't get up. I didn't turn on the bright lights in her stall, since enough soft light came from the aisle lights for me to see each mare clearly enough. There was no need to disturb the resting horses with the brighter lights in their individual stalls until they were needed.

I shivered in spite of my thick jacket and tried not to worry. Maybe Cliff's car had gotten a flat tire or something. Even the fancy cars Cliff drove must get flat tires, like the ordinary cars most people drove. Most of Cliff's cars, and he seemed to have a brand-new one every time he came by, looked like sharks with mean faces, too mean to let their tires go flat—

I moved on to the next big stall. This mare was lying down, too, but her bedding was tossed around her as though she'd recently been up and moving restlessly. She'd had several foals before, all of them raised right here at the farm and growing up to be useful winners at the racetrack. Her latest yearling had brought a very good price at the Saratoga sales. "Take it easy, Pamela," I whispered to the mare. "Give us a nice colt this time, just like last year's, okay?"

Pamela was a plain bay, a daughter of the great sire Princequillo, and was the only one of three waiting broodmares that belonged to our farm. The chestnut and the brown belonged to outside clients. They'd come, as mares often did at breeding farms, to have their foals and then to be bred to one of our stallions. The Thoroughbred breeding season was short, and each mare would go to the stallion within a month of foaling. This way it wouldn't be necessary for the mares to travel to a new, strange stable with their newborn foals for their next breeding.

Cam and I had helped Dad with the new foals for years. It was always a terrific responsibility—newborn foals are so terribly fragile—but we enjoyed working with them, and we were good at it, and we knew we could always call the veterinarian whenever we needed advice or professional assistance.

All of our stallions had been sold by Dad, except for

the best of them and our favorite, Rondelay, sired by Round Table. Year after year Rondelay had been bred to all kinds of mares, and his foals were consistently good.

We had other horses, too, of course. The whole long aisle of the main stable held a number of them, from unbroken yearlings that we hoped would turn out to be good enough for the big summer sales to come, to our resting young racehorse, a colt named Glory Now. And Jimmy had three of our two-year-olds with him in training for the racetrack. They were good horses and they'd probably pay their way with their winnings, but not one of them looked sensationally exciting, which was tough. We sure could have used the money.

Cam and I were doing the best we could. We'd closed the other barns and stables on the farm after Dad had died almost six months before. Even by then, though, too many of the outer stalls had been empty in the yearling barn and the stallion barn, which once had held five first-class stallions, the broodmare barn, the stable for broodmares without foals, and the separate stable for visiting mares. We'd bolted the doors of the empty barns, latched the shutters tight against the windows, and watched the grass grow shaggy at the unused doorsills, while we promised ourselves we'd open them again as soon as we could, when things changed at the farm for the better. In the meantime, having the horses that were left all together in one stable, under a single roof, made it easier for the two of us to care for them.

I opened the door to the tack room and switched on the lights. The saddles and bridles hung on their racks in waiting silence, throwing familiar friendly shadows. The room was warm—it had its own heating and humidity control system—and it was scented with the glorious smell of fine leather, conditioning oils, and metal polishes. The lights glowed on golden brass fittings and silvery burnished bits. At the back of the long room were the racks of blankets in our blue and white stable colors, cabinets and shelves holding bandages and leg wraps for shipping, and all the heavy trunks filled with the countless odds and ends essential to running a big stable.

Everything, as always, was folded or wrapped and neatly stored in its place. I took the shipping bandages and sheets of cotton padding I needed to protect Rosie's legs for her trip in the van and went back down the silent aisle to her stall.

Rosie was asleep, flat out on her side. She waggled one of her long ears and opened her eyes as I slid her stall door open.

"Get up, Rosie," I said to her gently. Her only response was to close her eyes again. I patted her neck and tugged lightly on her mane. Rosie made popping sounds with her lips but didn't even bother to raise her head. I had to go get the halter that was hanging in its place by her door and put it on her head, scolding her lovingly, before she finally stretched and sighed and surged lazily to her feet.

She stood amiably while I wrapped her legs and brushed away the wisps of straw that had been caught in her mane and tail.

"I don't understand any of this, either," I said to the gentle mare, "but we'll find out eventually. I guess."

I put a fresh blue and white stable sheet on her and gave her a hug after I'd buckled it into place. I brought her an armload of hay to eat to keep her awake and went to look at the broodmares again.

The closed-circuit television camera eyes stared blindly into their stalls. We'd been so excited when they'd first been installed three years before. The idea was marvelous. The night watchman could wait in the office, checking the mares due to foal just by looking at the little television screen. Most foalings were reasonably uneventful, but if something went wrong, it went wrong in a hurry. Someone always had to be on the alert, and Dad was always called by the watchman at the very first signs of labor.

But now, like so many things at the farm, the small cameras no longer worked properly. And there was no money to have them repaired. Their blank eyes reflected the lights—constant reminders of what used to be.

Those were the days when the farm was doing well. Our yearlings were eagerly spoken for, and those we reserved to send to the important sales went for mind-bending prices. Dad was tall and happy and proud, a big man with sandy hair and a smiling face, warm blue eyes that always welcomed friends and strangers, and a reputation as a horseman and breeder of Thoroughbreds among the very best.

Then Mother had died suddenly. Cam and I saw the changes in Dad right away. We all missed Mom terribly and did what we could, but the joy was gone for him. Our lovely white house, surrounded by Mom's bright flower gardens, slowly grayed outside to match the gray feeling that had crept inside all the rooms. One by one the help drifted off. The gardener quit when Dad never paid any attention to the gardens, the young helper lost interest and left, and Dad didn't even seem to notice they'd gone. One of the maids went away for a weekend and never came back, the other soon followed, and the cook gave up and gave notice.

Cam and I didn't mind. We shut off most of the rooms because no one went in them anymore, anyway. We opened the high-ceilinged living room with the doors that led out to the terrace, the library, and the dining

room only for the annual afternoon parties the farm always gave before the big yearling sales. We'd shift the
fading upholstery of the furniture into the shadows and
heap all the flowers we could find into odds and ends of
huge racing trophies from years past. Cam and I would
spend two days just polishing the things. We'd put them
on the tables in the opened rooms and then quickly shut
everything up again the very next day, letting the silver
vases and bowls darken with tarnish until we needed them
again.

Three

The horses and the stables were a different matter. For a while, Dad made sure the driveways were raked smooth every morning, as they'd always been; the brass fittings in the stable glittered with polish, and the white boards of the paddock fencing gleamed with fresh paint.

Until the money began to run out.

Dad had let some of our finest broodmares go at ridiculous prices. It had made no sense to us and we never did understand why. He sent many of the remaining mares out to stallions that were not proven to be successful sires—horses he would have dismissed with nothing more than a polite smile a few years before.

And then Glory Now was born at Thunder Rock. He was a bay colt, out of our mare Pamela, but sired by a horse Dad wouldn't have given stall room to, if he'd been thinking clearly. For some reason, Dad thought the new colt was so special that he refused to sell him as a yearling, even at a dizzying price. "We'll win the Derby with this colt, at the very least," Dad predicted. And for a long time, everybody believed him, mostly because we wanted to. The very idea brought some light back to his face, and it was impossible not to get caught up by his excitement.

The colt was hurt before he got to the races, as so often happens, no matter how carefully they're handled. Jimmy had Glory in training with his string of other young racehorses in Florida in the early spring, and called to tell Dad that the colt had bumped a leg schooling from the starting gate and cut a gash near a tendon. But the vets were working on it, and Jimmy hoped to have the colt back in training in a few weeks.

It didn't work that way. The leg was slow to heal. Glory missed the first big races for two-year-olds, but there was a lot of talk about him in the papers. When Jimmy at last was able to start slow workouts with the colt again in the early mornings, the sportswriters and television reporters decided they liked the way Glory Now looked and moved. So on the days when there wasn't much else in the racing world to write about, they wrote about the promising young colt from Thunder Rock Farm.

Glory Now was a rich red bay with ink-black legs and dashing white markings on his face and just above each of his hoofs. He photographed well, posing like a movie star for anyone with a camera and putting on a noble look that people fell all over themselves to get on film. Glory was handsome and seemed always to be aware of it, though I heard Jimmy mutter once, under his breath, that the colt put on airs as though he was important, but hadn't done a single thing yet in his life to prove it.

I didn't pay any attention. Like everybody else, I was eagerly looking forward to his first race. Glory Now was going to change everything for us.

His workouts in the morning in the blue mists at Saratoga were suitably spectacular. As the day of his first race grew near, we saw him on almost every television sports show, galloping proudly through the shimmery early morning light, with his exercise rider looking just as proud on his back.

The day of his first race was full of bright skies and sunshine, and Glory, carrying the blue and white silks of our farm, won easily.

For the first time in a long while, Dad went to a celebration party that night.

Cam and I, worn out with excitement, went with Jimmy for a hamburger after he'd seen the horses settled in for the night.

"There's just one small problem," Jimmy said to us, studying the napkin in his hand. "I haven't got the heart to tell your father something I'd bet anything he already knows, only he doesn't want to face it. That fancy colt can't run fast enough to keep himself warm."

Cam raised her shocked face to Jimmy, hoping he was kidding. But he wasn't.

He ducked his head to avoid looking at Cam's anxious expression and poured too much milk into his coffee to give his hands something to do.

"Glory Now won today," Jimmy said. "But it wasn't much of a horse race. You two should know that just as well as your father, and you might as well admit it to yourselves. Face facts. He ran today against a bunch of horses who've been out there racing all season and getting tired and beaten pretty consistently. Glory was fresh, and I figured he could handle that particular race without too much disgrace. Which he did, and even made himself look like a real live racehorse. But did you think to look at the time it took him to do it?"

Jimmy looked up at Cam directly. "Quit kidding yourself. I know how badly your father needed to win a race, any race, but that's about all there's going to be."

"But Glory's times. In the morning workouts. Everybody's talking about them," I said, almost furiously, though I knew Jimmy wouldn't have told us such a thing about the horse if it wasn't so. "How come all the excitement? Newspapers? Television?"

"The horse is a morning glory, Stephany," Jimmy said flatly. "And that's all he'll ever be. Workouts to blow your mind in the mornings and races to make you want to blow your brains out in the afternoons. That's all he's good for—sizzling times for a furlong or two in the early morning to impress the rail birds and the secret timers, who've spread the word that this colt is something special. And then Glory's day is done. He won't put any effort into his running. He couldn't care less, he doesn't try, and this kind of horse doesn't win horse races. At least, not the important races that matter and that your dad needs so much."

The three of us sat in silence. Cam turned a spoon over and over on the tabletop. I stared out the window at the traffic going by.

"I must get your dad somehow to see the real truth about this colt," Jimmy said unhappily. "It's going to be hard. I know how he's been counting on this particular horse. And your dad hasn't been too well these last months, has he?"

Cam's pale hair slipped down to cover her cheeks.

21

"That's right," she said. "Not for a while, not really. I don't think he's ever gotten over missing Mother. And lately—"

She shook her head a little. I didn't say anything. What was there to be said?

Jimmy put his hand out to cover Cam's. She stopped twisting the spoon and let her hand lie quietly clasped in his. I flipped my ponytail over my shoulder and started chewing thoughtfully on the end of it. But there was nowhere for my mind to go with its thinking. Facts were facts, and slow horses didn't win horse races. No matter how much it might have meant to Dad. Or how much it would have meant to the declining fortunes of Thunder Rock Farm.

Glory came down with colic a few nights later. The stomach pains of colic could be scary and sometimes mean all kinds of terrible problems, but his particular case was no big deal. The night watchman called Jimmy at once, the vets came quickly, and the colt was bright and perky by the very next morning. He was a greedy eater and had probably stuffed down his grain too fast at supper time. No damage was done. But it gave Jimmy a good excuse to keep the colt out of competition for a while— the last thing any of us wanted or needed for Dad or the farm just then was to let the silly colt get himself soundly beaten, which was bound to happen if he ran against any decent kind of racehorse.

I saw Jimmy talking to Dad, and then Dad gave an interview to an eager young sportswriter from a small newspaper, just before noon. Rumors spread wildly. By two o'clock, the television cameras were set up near the row of stalls. The word had gotten out; the TV people would get it all in time for the evening news programs, which Jimmy had clearly been counting on.

"The reporters have made Glory Now into a media hype," Jimmy told Cam and me with a shrug of his shoulders as we watched the crews set up their cameras. "I never tried to mislead them. I never told them this colt was more than he was—they chose to pick him out and make all the fuss. I've seen it happen before. We'll let them carry the rest of the story by themselves and make what they want of it, just as they've done up to now. This should give us a break and take the pressure off for a little while."

Four

Making sure there was a horse or two being led around in the background for atmosphere, Jimmy walked over to stand beside Dad and arranged his face in a seriously thoughtful expression. I stood over in the shade of the stable area, trying not to giggle and thinking all he needed for the final dramatic touch was to take his cap off and twist it sadly in his hands.

"Ladies and gentlemen," he said, looking sorrowfully into the camera, "it seems you've heard of Glory Now's illness last night. Thanks to immediate attention and the skillful veterinary care he was given, the colt appears well enough today. But it would be unforgivable to threaten the welfare of this colt, or the promise of his future in racing, by ignoring the warning signs that might lead to far more serious problems."

Jimmy bowed his head slightly toward Dad. "Mr. Reed, who of course you know bred and raised the colt and owns Thunder Rock Farm, is the one to ask about the immediate plans for his horse."

Dad imitated Jimmy's serious expression. "Sorry as I am to disappoint those who have looked forward to seeing my colt run again this summer, we must keep what is best for the horse in mind. There's always next year. We've decided not to risk further stress for him now. It might well threaten his entire racing career, even his very life, to continue his training for the rest of this season. It isn't often an owner and trainer have the good fortune to handle a great colt of such promise—" and so on. I stopped listening and went to pat the little black and white Russell terrier that belonged to one of the exercise riders. I couldn't help wondering, a little uneasily, if Dad really believed what he was saying about Glory Now's wonderful future.

The television interviewers shouted questions. It hadn't been much of a racing year. Most of the horses that had caught the public eye during the early races had broken down or had been beating each other, one way or another, all summer long, and fresh racing news was scarce. Because of this, the interviews with Jimmy and Dad were on almost every channel on the evening news, along with earlier clips of Glory flying along in morning workouts and winning his one race.

We loaded the young horse into the farm van very early the next morning for the long trip home. Cam was driving and I was going with her both to keep her company and to lend a hand if there were any problems with the colt. Early as it was, there were cameras clicking and whirring and grinding from all directions as we led Glory Now out of his stall.

I worked at keeping a solemn expression as I covered the colt's gleaming coat with a light traveling sheet. He looked as sharp as a tack, of course. There wasn't a thing in the world the matter with him, and he danced out to the van as though he'd never had an off day in his life, fit and ready to run that very day.

Jimmy led Glory into the van and shut him and his glossy coat and happy spirit away from the cameras.

Dad stayed on at Saratoga for the rest of the meeting, with everyone full of kindness and welcoming him to their boxes and dinner parties. Dad always had loved the Saratoga race meetings, and he seemed more his old bright self while he was there, surrounded by the friends and all the horse world he loved.

Jimmy had other horses racing at Saratoga, so he had to stay, too. But Cam and I had no problems. Our trip home was uneventful. The colt bounded out of the van when we got home, looking as glorious as ever. We thanked the temporary help we'd hired to care for the farm while we'd been gone and they left, relieved to see that the colt looked well and shining in spite of all the worrying news they'd heard. His name went up on a brass plate beside his door, and all kinds of people drifted in and out during the next several weeks to admire him and sympathize with his shortened racing season.

I found Cam cleaning tack one day, her face flushed in the steam from the hot soapy water.

"First time in my life I ever saw such a fuss made over a horse that hasn't done one single darned thing," she said. "It really is kind of funny."

"Never mind." I went to get the bridle I needed. "Dad thinks all this is great, and maybe by next spring Glory *will* find out what running's all about. Probably he's just a late bloomer. Maybe he just needed extra time and he'll be a smasher of a racehorse as a three-year-old."

"He'd better be a late bloomer," said Cam through the steam, looking serious again. "We haven't got anything else coming along that shows much promise, and we sure need something."

Thanks to all the publicity Glory had collected, at

least people were talking about our farm and our horses again. During the next few weeks, we sold off two brood-mares of uninteresting bloodlines and a young filly that never was going to amount to a whole lot, and things looked considerably brighter than they had for a while. Media hype or not, Glory had made the name of our farm fashionable again. At least for a little while.

The next rotten blow fell at the beginning of September. Cam was packed and ready to go back to college, where she was studying nursing. Dad had convinced her to go back. He insisted that he and I and some part-time help could handle the horses without her; her education was too important to give up. Just before she was planning to leave, Cam was in the stable office looking for a pedigree form in the files for a client and discovered by accident how few of our good mares were due to have foals the next year. The paperwork was done, contracts had been signed for different sires, but Dad somehow had not gotten around to sending the mares out to the breeding farms.

This was the worst kind of news. The mares were producers, or supposed to be, bringing income to the farm through the sales of their foals. No foals, no money. Simple as that.

Dad didn't seem to care. We never knew if he understood what harm he'd done by forgetting to send the mares away. If money had been so tight, he could at least have bred our mares to Rondelay right here at Thunder Rock and raised some nice youngsters.

Cam quietly unpacked her suitcases, made excuses to the college and to Dad, and gently took over the running of the farm. Dad didn't seem to mind. We weren't sure how much he really noticed. He went off often to visit friends at neighboring breeding farms and talked a lot about horses of years ago, while Cam stayed up until all hours, night after night, trying to balance the books and straighten out the neglected records.

The farm clearly was teetering on the edge of disaster. We had to let two of the grooms go, and then the last. Cam got a part-time job as a secretary-typist in the afternoons, to make some extra money, and I came straight home from school every day to help with the stable work. Cam would wait until the school bus dropped me off at the farm entrance before leaving for her job, so there'd always be one of us on the place to watch over the horses. It was hectic, but it was working. We thought we were doing well enough.

Glory pranced and glowed in the high-fenced stallion paddock near his stall every bright day. Dad watched him for hours at a time, pretty well ignoring all the other horses and the problems on the farm. Clearly, to Dad, Glory was still the horse to turn everything around, and only part of his wonderful future was to be running in the Kentucky Derby next spring. And winning it, of course. Even I started to believe in the colt's promise again because I wanted to so much. Trainers had been wrong about horses in the past. Surely Jimmy was wrong about this one.

"Jimmy knows a good horse when he sees one," Cam reminded me whenever my hopes began to rise.

"Did he ever tell Dad what he really thinks about Glory and his future?" I asked her—she saw Jimmy a lot more than I did.

"Not yet," Cam said after a moment's silence. "He doesn't want to be the one to burst the last dream Dad seems to have to hold on to. But I think he should. Waiting might just make things worse."

But Dad never knew. Or, if he'd guessed, he certainly never said. It was on the short drive over to Jimmy's farm one morning to talk about the exciting training plans for Glory during the coming year that Dad's car drifted gently to a stop by an old oak that marked a turn in the road. The doctors said it was his heart and that he'd died peacefully at the wheel.

CHAPTER

Five

The weeks that followed were sad and bewildering beyond belief. Lots of our friends and relatives suggested we sell the farm, and an aunt I barely knew offered to take me in while Cam went back to college. Aunt Helen lived in an apartment in a city halfway across the country. Cam and I both were horrified, though we did manage to thank her politely.

The very idea of living with strangers—and in a city,

at that—was enough to make me feel sick. I'd miss Cam and the horses and the farm so much that it would be unbearable. There was a little insurance money, and if Cam kept on working and got a full-time job during my summer vacation when I'd be able to stay with the horses all day, she might be able to manage to finish nursing school at night. We could probably take in a few brood-mares to board, and, if we worked very hard with the good horses we had left, we hoped fiercely that things would get better in a few short years.

I handled as much of the farm work as I could. Every now and then one of my friends from school would come to help. Sometimes a neighbor would lend a hand. Our tractor was just about old enough to vote and broke down at intervals, but somehow we kept things going. It helped to know how proud Mom and Dad would have been to know their daughters were fighting out a working future for Thunder Rock.

I went out riding on Rosie whenever I had a few minutes to spare. Riding her always made things seem a little better. But she hadn't been getting the attention she was used to. There'd been just too much to get done and not enough hours in each day.

As I waited for Jimmy's van and for Cam to come home, I flung my arms around Rosie's neck and buried my face in the hollow of her clean, sweet shoulder. Both of us missed our long, happy rides together from the days that now seemed so long ago.

"It'll be better soon," I said to her, hoping I believed it. "This is all just temporarily a tough time."

I went back into the office and stared out of the window smeared with rain. My own blurry face stared back at me. My hair was pulled back in a ponytail, as it usually was, and it was the same light blond as Cam's. Our eyes weren't exactly the same color. Hers were more violet, as Mother's had been. Mine were more blue, like Dad's. . . . My mind wandered, remembering, until at last I saw headlights and heard Jimmy's van crunching up the drive. I hurried to open the wide stable doors.

"Cam back yet?" Jimmy said as he swung out of the van.

"No. And no word, either."

Jimmy looked anxious, but didn't say anything more. In silence we ran the van ramp out to the ground and put the ramp wings in place.

Rosie looked mildly surprised to be led outside into the dark, but the rain had stopped and she walked without trouble into the van and backed up into the narrow shipping stall with her usual common sense. Within a few minutes, Jimmy was getting back into the van's cab.

"I'll tell you about this later, Stephany," he called to

me. "I don't have time to explain now. It's a little complicated."

"Sure," I said. I shrugged my shoulders. The way things had been going, it was almost impossible to be surprised at anything that happened anymore. There wasn't much else I could say. But I couldn't resist shouting at the back of the receding van, "You take good care of Rosie," though I knew very well Jimmy couldn't hear me. Just as I knew he would take good care of her, no matter what I said.

I rolled the doors shut. The stable seemed terribly quiet and I felt more alone than ever. I thought of calling my best friend just to talk to a friendly voice for a little while, until I remembered what time it was. I didn't think either Lyn or her parents would be thrilled by a phone call in the middle of the night, just to chat. I turned to a country music station on the radio in the office, with the sound on low, and that helped a little. I went back to look at the broodmares.

The pretty chestnut mare was up on her feet, turning restlessly in her straw bed. She started to lie down and then walked in a circle in her stall, stopping only to turn her head every now and then to look at her sides.

I'd been with mares having their foals countless times, but this time was different—I'd never been totally alone. My hands were sweaty with nervousness, even though I was shivering at the same time. But at least I knew what to watch for and what to do. I comforted myself with the thought of the vet's number taped beside the office phone and wondered if I should call him.

I hated to wake him for nothing. The chestnut mare had only just started to show signs of foaling, and I expected Cam any minute. She'd certainly be home soon.

I put the mare's halter on and made soothing sounds, patting her encouragingly on her shining neck. She nuzzled my arm gently, turned around once, and lay down again.

Her contractions grew strong very quickly. I glanced at my watch and made a mental note of the time.

The mare broke into a sweat. I knelt in the straw beside her—no signs yet of the expected foal. I tried to track it inside its mother with a gentle hand, trying to tell how close it was to being born, but I felt no more than empty warmth.

I dried my hands on a towel from the stack of clean ones outside the stall and waited.

The minutes ticked by. The mare was straining, but there was still no sign of the foal. I started to the door. I wanted to call the vet.

But the moment I started to leave the stall, the mare got up uneasily. "I'll only be gone one little minute," I said to her, but this didn't help. Instead, as I went outside the door, she started spinning in wild circles.

I plunged back into her stall and put a hand on her

halter. The mare quieted down at once, sighed a little, and lay down again in the soft straw.

I waited to let her calm down, then tried to go to the telephone once more. But she jumped anxiously to her feet when I tried to leave her stall and started spinning hysterically as she had before.

I calmed the mare again with my voice and by stroking her shoulder, and she lay down again.

Her contractions were so strong they were almost violent. I checked the foal's progress and froze. I'd never felt so many tiny hoofs, and no signs of the foal's head anywhere.

Surprised and confused, I felt carefully, trying to track at least one leg back to the unborn foal. No hope.

I heard the stable door open and, with a dizzy feeling of relief, heard Camilla saying, "Good night, Cliff," in an icy voice. I called to her over the sound of Cliff's throaty little car driving away. "I'm in here, Cam, with the chestnut mare. Something's not right, and she won't let me leave her. I haven't even been able to call the vet."

The high heels of her gold sandals tapped quickly on the stable aisle as Cam hurried to the open stall door. "Let me see," she said. The folds of her pale blue evening dress spread out around her on the golden straw as she knelt beside the mare. With a quick, reassuring smile to me, Cam began to feel for the expected foal.

"I think there are twenty in there. At least," I said, exaggerating somewhat wildly. "It's all a jumble of legs. I never felt so many."

"Two foals, anyway," Cam said, nodding. "She's having twins. Get to the phone and call Dr. Bailey. It's going to be quite a job, getting all this straightened out."

The mare was happy to have Cam stay with her. I ran to the phone and called the vet. Mrs. Bailey answered and said the doctor was at another farm with a difficult foaling but would call when he had the chance. His assistant was out with him—the expected foal they were working with was sired by Seattle Slew and half the foreign owners had been calling in a frenzy, the insurance agents were on their way, and it looked like a long night. I called the next two doctors on our emergency list, but they were out on calls, too. Their answering services said they'd try to reach them. I went back to the stall to tell Cam.

"Let's see if we can get this mare on her feet," said Cam. "If we can get her walking, it may slow down the labor until we can get help."

I brought her a lead rope, which she clipped to the mare's halter. Cam stood up, pushing her taffeta skirts back out of the way impatiently, and clucked encouragingly to the mare.

37

The horse's eyes were a little wild and she seemed confused, but at Cam's insistent but gentle urging, she scrambled awkwardly to her feet.

I took the lead rope and led the mare into the wide stable aisle, while Cam hurried to the office to find something to put on her feet warmer and more suitable than the gold sandals with their high heels and narrow straps.

Her soft, white fur jacket, cut down from a coat Dad had given Mother years ago, was flung on top of a bale of hay. The ring and bracelets Cam had yanked off before coming to the mare lay like little crystals of light on the pretty coat lining. I snatched a bent horse blanket pin from the pocket of my jacket and pinned them to the coat.

"Thanks, Stephany." Cam was coming back from the office. "Party time's over for now."

Cam was wearing a pair of fur-lined boots and she'd put an old down jacket over her evening gown. Her bright hair was wrapped in a quick knot on top of her head to keep it out of her way.

Together we tugged at the chestnut mare's halter and patted her as she walked, and I talked to her in a babble of encouraging words that didn't necessarily make sense but helped my nervousness as well as the mare's.

"What are we going to do?" I said to Cam at last, trying not to have my words come out in a frightened wail.

"Maybe we should call Jimmy," Camilla said. "He's foaled a lot of mares. He worked with Dr. Bailey all one foaling season—"

"He's not home," I said. "He's gone out with the van somewhere." I started to tell Cam about Rosie, but just then the mare flung herself stubbornly down in the stable aisle and refused absolutely to get to her feet again.

"We're going to have to figure out a way to do this ourselves," said Cam. "She's clearly got twins in there, all tangled up and both trying to get themselves born at the same time without enough room. We'll have to try to sort them out one way or another. That's all there is to it."

CHAPTER

Six

"Have you ever seen twin horses born, anywhere?" I said
anxiously. We'd never had them before at Thunder Rock.
Cam just shook her head. Of course we knew about twin
foals, both trying to be born at the same time. Not such
an incredibly unusual situation. Foaling them sounded
reasonably simple in the pages of the farm's veterinary
books, which Cam and I had read so often we knew most
of them almost by heart.

It wasn't simple. First, we had to coax the sweating mare back into her stall. Then, closing her eyes in concentration, Cam went to work. "This one first, I think," she said. I understood what she meant. One foal would have to wait its turn, pushed gently back into the mare while Cam tried to give the other one room to be born.

I never knew how we did it. I guess we were so desperate that it just plain had to work. I stayed by the mare's head to reassure her. She would strain and Cam would wait, her lips set in a tight line of concern, until the contractions eased. Then she'd sort things out inside the mare as well as she could and try to remember which pair of tiny hoofs belonged to which foal.

Daylight began to turn the stable windows to dirty gray. The mare looked tired. Cam's face was pale but determined, and suddenly, with a great rush, the first tiny red-gold foal was lying in the deep gold of the straw.

"One down, one to go," Cam said triumphantly. I rubbed the steaming newborn baby with towels, pressing on its ribs vigorously to help it take its first breaths of air. I wiped its small, sweet face with a clean towel, feeling the glorious relief so familiar and so wonderful at seeing the new life safely beginning. In spite of the long time its trip into the world had taken, the newborn foal seemed okay to me, and I chuckled and chirped to it fondly while Cam kept her eyes on the weary mare.

41

Cam sat back on her heels and took a deep breath. "The mare's resting," she said. "I wonder if she thinks it's all over. She's in for a terrific surprise, if she thinks she's done with all this."

The skirts of Cam's long blue dress were wet and stained, but she paid no attention. The new foal raised its head on its wobbly neck and blinked its enormous, dark eyes.

"It's pretty," I reported. "Lots of white markings, like its mother."

"That's nice," Cam said warmly but a little absently. She was watching the mare's flanks as new contractions started. "Here comes number two."

The second foal slipped out easily and the mother lay quietly in the straw, looking dreamy and contented, while Cam and I tended to the new arrival.

I turned on the overhead heat lamps that were mounted in each foaling stall. We rubbed both new foals with more clean towels. Their short, fuzzy coats were beginning to dry nicely and both of them seemed to be breathing well. They looked a lot alike, which wasn't always the way with twins, from the pictures I'd seen. Both of the new foals were fillies, and both had pretty white markings, just like their mother, and just like their immortal grandfather, Secretariat.

Cam and I knew the owners would be disappointed. A lot of people believed that twins seldom made good racehorses. Usually they were considered too small or not strong enough to be winners on the track. But that wasn't our problem; our first duties were to the mare and her foals.

The first foal born was soon struggling to get up on her thin, quivering little legs, gathering fresh strength with every effort. The second didn't look much interested even in trying.

I stood up and leaned against the oak-lined walls of the stall. I looked at the two foals out of eyes that felt as though they'd been dipped in sand. It had been an exhausting few hours, but just part of a long night that wasn't over yet.

"I'd better go check those other two mares," I said. "It's been a while since either of us had the chance."

Cam nodded, and I slipped out as quietly as I could.

The dark brown mare was down and was clearly in active labor. I hurried to report to Cam, then went back to the mare. After days and nights of waiting, everything was happening at once. It was this mare's first foal and she was puzzled as to what was happening to her. She looked tense and worried, but everything seemed to be going normally, so I stayed with her, wondering why some mares liked to have people with them when they foaled, and others would go to almost any extreme to deliver their foals alone. There was no answer to this kind of question, but it kept my tired mind busy while I stroked the mare's head until she relaxed. Her foal was born a few minutes later—a big, handsome colt. He started to breathe and move his head right away and even tried to get up on his funny little hoofs before his coat was half dry.

"I don't see any problems with this one," I called to Camilla with relief. The colt was by one of the most currently popular racehorse sires, and I was smugly pleased at how delighted its owners would be when we had the chance the next morning to call them and tell them the good news.

This was before the colt stood up and went over to his mother to try to nurse. The mare let out a squeal of protest and took a kick at her new baby that could well have demolished him if I hadn't shoved him swiftly out of the way.

"Neat," I said to the mare. "Just what we needed after a night like this." I had to call to Cam for help; in one stall we had a tired mare with twins, one of which wasn't trying very hard to face the challenge of her new life, and in the next stall a frantic mare who had no idea of what this strange new and damp little creature was, or how it came to be suddenly in the same stall with her. And she clearly was planning not to have anything to do with it.

Time went by in a haze of worry. Finally, with Cam hanging grimly onto the reluctant mare's head with a double twist in the lead rope, and with me guiding the foal, he was able to take his first gulps of milk. The chocolate mare sighed at last and rolled her eyes toward her new foal. Cam kept one hand on the halter but let the suspicious mare turn her head. We watched her cautiously as she poked at the foal with her muzzle. The last thing in the world we needed was to have the mare make a dive at her baby and mash him flat with her forehoofs. But after the first few minutes, the mare gave a low, sweet sound deep in her throat and began to lick her foal.

Even though things looked a whole lot better, we didn't dare leave the stall until the colt at last had his fill of milk, swayed sleepily, and curled up for a nap in the soft bed of straw. We waited until the mare had gone over to him, sniffed him all over, and seemed happy to stand peacefully beside him.

Cam blew a strand of her hair from her forehead with a puff of relief. We went back to the twins again. The second filly had finally discovered how to stand up, but when she tried to nurse, she was quickly shoved out of the way by her more aggressive sister. Cam picked up the weaker foal and held her gently in her arms as she groped for her mother's milk. I kept the stronger filly away. It took a while, but eventually the foal Cam was holding found what she was after, and the sweet sound of nursing filled the anxious silence in the stall.

45

"We may have to give this little one a bottle now and then to help her get a better start," said Cam. "What about Pamela? Is she going to foal now, too? We've been watching these mares for so long—how many weeks has it been? I've lost track—and here they are, all coming at once."

"I don't know," I said. "I've looked at her two or three times, in between the others, but nothing was actually happening. She sure looks due any time now, though."

Cam moved silently down the aisle, glanced at Pamela, and nodded. "Not long, I think. But maybe time for us to have a cup of coffee. Or something. I'll get some kind of a breakfast together for us if you'll feed the other horses."

I gave the row of hungry horses their grain and hay, filled their water buckets, and left them eating contentedly while Cam and I had the breakfast she brought out to the office. I couldn't remember when scrambled eggs and English muffins had ever tasted so good.

"That Cliff," said Cam as she buttered her muffin. "I'm terribly sorry I was so late getting back, but he had trouble with his car halfway home. At least, that's what he said. I got so angry, knowing you were here alone with the mares, that his car had a sudden miraculous recovery. We did have a good time at the dance, but in some ways he's a very selfish person, I'm afraid."

CHAPTER

Seven

Cam began mixing a formula of evaporated milk, water, sweet corn syrup, and lime water in a baby bottle for the weaker twin foal. I went to check Pamela again.

She had been waiting impatiently for her morning grain when I'd fed all the horses a short while ago. I'd left her with her muzzle buried deep in her feed tub, eating hungrily, but half her breakfast was unfinished and Pamela was down in the stall, starting to have her new foal with a minimum of fuss, as she always did.

I went to get Cam and we stayed quietly outside the mare's stall. There was no need for us to interfere unless we were needed.

In less than fifteen minutes, there was a big, handsome foal in the stall with its mother. Cam went in to rub its head with a towel and make sure it was able to breathe properly.

"It's a splendid colt, and everything looks just fine," she said. Pamela was still lying down. She turned her head toward her new foal and nickered to him gently. He answered with a funny little squeak and began moving his incredibly long, thin legs haphazardly, as though he wasn't sure what made them move at all.

"Good," Cam said, with a wide smile. "This one will be up and nursing before we know it."

We waited, leaning contentedly against the stall, happy with the wonder that never lost its enchantment, no matter how many foals we'd seen born. It was always new and special, time after time, watching each tiny new spark of life start burning with a kind of steady flame as the foal grew stronger with each passing moment.

He staggered to his feet, fell over his own front legs, which he hadn't thought to uncross, and tottered back to his feet again quickly. The mare rose to her own feet and turned to nuzzle and lick her new foal. There were more little squeaks from the colt and soft welcoming sounds from his mother, and within a few minutes he was nursing happily.

"We'll leave them for a little while," said Cam. "What a marvelous mare she is."

We went back to the office and Cam flung herself down on the couch by the window. "It's been quite a night, Steph. What with this and that . . . ."

At last I had the chance to tell her about Rosie and how Jimmy had insisted on picking her up at once, without explaining why. Cam just shook her head with a yawn. "Probably he needed to borrow a gentle older horse to travel along with a young one."

She closed her eyes. "Don't let me go to sleep," she said. "There's too much to do. . . ." Her voice drifted into silence.

I moved the two cats, covered Cam with the plaid blankets, and turned off the office lights. The sun was rising. Moving as quietly as I could, I took the baby bottle Cam had been mixing and put it in the small pan of steaming water heating on the hot plate beside Dad's old desk. It only took a few minutes to warm. I switched off the heat and went to see the new foals.

The weaker twin wasn't doing well at all. She was lying almost motionless, stretched out at the side of the big stall, while her bigger sister nursed busily and took all her mother's attention.

I sat down beside the little foal, crossed my legs comfortably, and propped her head in my lap. "Come on," I said to her. "You've got to try a little harder." I shook a few drops of formula from the bottle into my hand and rubbed them on the foal's tiny muzzle. She showed no interest at all.

I pushed the soft rubber nipple of the bottle into her mouth through the side of her lips. It was a complicated business, trying to squeeze some of the formula into her mouth and hold onto her head and the bottle, all at the same time, and it seemed to take forever. One of my arms started to shake with tiredness. The sun rose higher outside the stall window. The stronger foal lay down for a nap and the mother nibbled calmly at her hay.

"*Try,*" I said almost furiously to the foal in my lap. "You can't give up. I won't let you—" I could feel tears stinging the backs of my eyes, and they hurt. I was so tired after the long, busy night that I ached all over in bones I'd never known existed before. The tiny, perfect little foal lay still, her head unmoving except for the flutter of her small nostrils as she breathed in light, shallow breaths. Occasionally she blinked her eyes or moved her small ears a little, but that was all.

I pressed more formula out of the bottle into the foal's still mouth. In spite of the heat lamps, she felt cold to me. I put the bottle down, struggled out of my jacket, placed it over her, and poked the bottle back into her mouth again.

I don't know what started things working. I watched, almost unbelieving and hardly daring to hope, as the muscles of the foal's golden throat began to move. Her eyes opened wider, she gave a small wiggle, and began to suck on the bottle at last. The bubbles in the bottle whispered and sang as the formula disappeared. Three ounces gone—four— I hardly dared blink as I watched the measuring lines on the bottle show the changes as the tiny foal nursed.

Suddenly the filly gave an enormous sigh, her head sagged back onto the straw, and her eyes closed.

"She's dead," I said out loud, turning frantically to look at the unheeding mare chewing on her hay behind me. This time my eyes did fill with tears and they ran down my cheeks. Some of them fell on the bottle I was still holding in my hand. It was such a sad ending after so much caring. I put the bottle down in the straw and put my hand sorrowfully on the filly's white star.

She moved her head a little and sighed again, stretching her long legs out strongly in the rustling straw. I bent over her, this time laughing and crying at the same time. She wasn't dead at all. Full of good milk, she'd fallen into a deep, contented sleep.

I struggled to my feet, hoping my legs would hold me

51

up. I smiled at the mare, the two red-gold fillies, and the sun-filled window. I even grinned at a wisp of gray cobweb high in a corner of the stall, though I made a note in my mind it would be gone before noon.

I put my jacket back on, pulled the light little foal across the straw until she was in the warmest spot under the heat lamps, and silently left the stall.

I rinsed the sticky bottle under the hot water tap at the back sink near the tack room, left it to soak, and started to clean out stalls.

It had become a beautiful morning, unusually warm for early February. I turned most of the horses out into the paddocks and pastures and left the outside doors of their stalls open to the sunlight. Rondelay was happy to be led out to his own paddock. Glory was bucking and plunging impatiently in his stall, and it took me a while to get his halter on his head, but I didn't want to wake Cam for help unless I really had to. Eventually, I was able to fasten the buckle and snap on the lead shank, and Glory and I took turns dragging each other out to his paddock where I turned him free with relief, ducking back out of the way as he kicked and spun in the fresh morning. I watched him for a few minutes as the sunlight shot little red flames of highlights in his gleaming coat. He arched his powerful neck and skimmed across the paddock grass in a sweeping trot, tossing his silky black mane and carrying his tail like a banner. He was a beautiful horse, no question about it. "All show and no go," I said to him a little bitterly. "If you could only run as well as you look, we'd all be in clover."

I turned my back and plodded toward the chores still waiting in the stable. I unzipped my jacket and turned my face up to the sun. I was tired, but proud of the long night's work and the four lovely foals safely launched into their new world.

It was almost half-past nine. The boy who was supposed to help with the heavy stable work hadn't arrived, though he was supposed to be at the farm at eight. It seemed that he'd chosen still another day not to show up, but he'd done this so often in the past that it was no surprise.

I wished we could afford just one good full-time groom, but it was out of the question for now. Still, we were managing pretty well, I thought, and I was delighted when the tractor started after only three tries. I emptied the soiled straw bedding from the stalls into the manure trailer and was starting to put down fresh bedding when Cam came out of the office, looking guilty and cross.

"You shouldn't have let me sleep like that, with so much still to be done," she said. "Are the mares and foals all right?"

"No problem. I've looked in on them a number of

times," I said. "Don't worry. I gave the one twin a bottle about an hour ago, and if you're looking for something to do, I'd think she probably needs another by now. She seemed so hungry. With a little help, I think she's going to be okay, after all. The others look fine."

Cam nodded and went to see for herself. I finished the last of the stalls.

Cam gave a fresh bottle to the little twin foal and went into the house at last to shower and change out of her limp evening dress.

"Your turn," she said when she came back in jeans and a sweater. "You've done more than enough. Go get cleaned up and rest for a while. I'll call and see if I can scare up a vet to check the mares and the new babies."

CHAPTER

Eight

My shoes whispered over the gravel drive to the path that led to the kitchen door of the house. We seldom used the front door anymore. There were two tiny but comfortable maids' rooms and a bath at the back of the house near the kitchen. Cam and I had taken them over for our own. It was nice not to have to walk through the dim halls and front rooms of the house, which were so full of memories, every day. I took a long, hot, glorious bath and fell onto my bed.

When I woke up an hour later, I made myself two peanut butter sandwiches and carried a banana and an apple with me as I hurried back to the stable.

Dr. Bailey's veterinary mobile unit was parked in the stable driveway. I left the sandwiches and fruit in the office and hurried to make sure everything was all right. The doctor was just finishing his examination of the last of the three mares as I let myself quietly into the stall.

Dr. Bailey looked worn out. He was too thin, anyway, and his dark eyes looked darker than ever with deep shadows around them. I supposed Cam and I must look the same. Foaling time was a tremendously tense and tiring time for the vets and everyone else responsible for the welfare of the broodmares and their new foals at all the breeding farms. But on their success depended the very existence of the farms and their hopes and most of their income for the entire year ahead.

"I'm sorry I couldn't come when you called last night," he was saying to Cam. "But we had a few problems." From the look on his face, I guessed they'd lost the Seattle Slew foal, and Cam told me later it was true.

Dr. Bailey stopped a second time at the stall of the chestnut mare with the twins. Both the foals looked lively and much brighter than they had the night before. The two of them were even beginning to try to play a little in the deep straw of the stall. It was fun to watch them experimenting with their first attempts when they still weren't very steady on their feet.

"It would probably be good to go on bottle-feeding the one filly for several more days," Dr. Bailey said. "Or even longer. Twin or not, it would be a real shame to lose her. But you've sure managed to give her a good start. Have you told the owners yet?"

Cam laughed a little bitterly. "I called them this morning. They were furious and told me I should have let the weaker one die. I told them it wasn't my decision to make and I wouldn't do it anyway, under any circumstances. If anybody sends me a mare to foal, and she's carrying twins, then she'll have live twins, if I can manage. But it sure was tricky. What a tangle they were in."

"You two young ladies did a good job." Dr. Bailey smiled at me. "Keep up the good work. You certainly hit the jackpot last night, with three mares and four foals. Must have kept you a little busy. What have you got still to come? You've quite a band of broodmares here."

"That's the lot for this year," Cam said, trying to sound matter-of-fact to hide her disappointment. The rest of our good mares were out wandering in the big back pasture when they should have been in the nearby paddocks, waiting their turns in the foaling stalls.

"There were a few mix-ups last year," Cam said carefully. "Dad wasn't well."

57

Dr. Bailey nodded tactfully. "Call me if you have any questions or problems with the ones born last night. Keep in touch."

Cam and I went into the office, and I saw she had the farm record books spread out on the desk. She made a notation of the veterinarian's visit, then went back to the columns of figures in another bound record book.

She was very quiet, with her head bowed over the pages. I offered her the apple, which she took with a murmured "thank you," and I looked at the numbers over her shoulder.

"That bad?" I said, looking at the bottom of the pages. The banana I was eating had begun to taste like dry ashes as the numbers in front of me sorted themselves out in my mind.

"Not exactly good," she said, pushing the book away and putting the pencil down. "Stephany, we're in some real kind of trouble. Dad has the broodmares booked to all kinds of different stallions this year, and we should probably get them sent on their way. I'm not all that crazy about some of the choices, but the booking fees have already been paid. We could cancel the actual breedings, but I don't think we'd get any of the deposits back. And they amount to quite a lot."

My mind searched wildly for something, anything,

comforting to say. "There's always Glory Now," I said eagerly. "Maybe he'll win some useful money for us this year. Maybe he really *will* win the Derby in the spring."

Cam just smiled. I put the half-finished banana down. Slippery as it was, I couldn't swallow what was left. I knew as well as she did that Jimmy was right and the colt was useless as a racehorse. Jimmy might have surprising ideas sometimes, but he'd never been wrong so far about any horse he'd had in training. And he'd never tried to fool us about the colt's potential.

"I've been looking into syndicating Rondelay," Cam said. "He'd stay here at Thunder Rock, of course—we'd only sell breeding shares—but there aren't many fancy breeders interested in a horse his age. And, nice as he is, none of his colts have brought millions at the sales, and that's where the big syndication money is going—"

"Put the books away for now," I said gently. "Tell me about the dance last night."

Cam laughed and bit into her apple. "That Cliff—he's impossible." I didn't say so out loud, but I couldn't have agreed more. I didn't like Cliff. I never had. He only saw Cam as a beautiful young thing to cling to his arm at all the right parties. I knew very well he wanted Cam to marry him, run his house with her special grace and charm, and spend the rest of her life being Mrs. Clifford Bennett. They'd own a few racehorses, I was sure of that.

But they'd all be bred and raised somewhere else by strangers, bought and sold at other people's convenience, and written off as tax shelters all over the world. Big deal. Cam would get to go to the fancier races and be at Cliff's side, smiling for the photographers, when the huge silver trophies were awarded in the winner's circle. In America, Canada, France, in England—all over Europe—it would all be the same for Cliff, as long as the horses ran in the fashionable races and won often enough to keep him happy. I wasn't at all sure it would be enough for Cam.

I listened politely and pretended to be interested as Cam told me about the dinner party before the dance, what different friends of hers had worn, and what they'd said.

I stared at the banana slowly turning brown on the desk beside the closed ledgers that held such dreary numbers. Who was I to judge? Maybe the life with Cliff was what Cam really wanted. No more worries about money, ever again. All the pretty clothes she wanted and certainly deserved. No more grubbing around in dark stables at night, scared, alone except for a much younger sister, tired, and foaling mares with not nearly enough help. She'd have Jaguars to drive instead of ancient pickup trucks and horse vans. Not to mention manure tractors.

I giggled. I wondered if anybody could drive a tractor

wearing a Dior original. Certainly, if anyone could, it would be Cam—

She was looking at me with a funny little smile. "That's enough about the life of carefree glamour," she said, jumping abruptly to her feet. "Let's go outside in the sun for a little while, while we have the chance. It will be time to feed the twin again soon."

Cam asked for a week off from her job. "I thought of requesting maternity leave," she said to me, laughing, "but I couldn't very well tell them at the office it was for horse babies."

An enormous box was delivered by a florist. It held several purple and white orchids, each one rigid and perfect, nested in clouds of soft green paper. They looked more like dead spiders than flowers to me. They were for Cam, with a note from Cliff. "Forgive me?" was all it said.

"Forget it," said Cam. She made a face as she looked down into the box. "Do you know, I think I hate these greenhouse flowers as much as Mother always did, but they cost so darned much, it doesn't seem right just to throw them away." The orchids ended up in a chipped pitcher in the kitchen and stood there curling their petals for a week until I finally tossed them into the trash.

I caught the school bus reluctantly the next morning.

I got all kinds of unpleasant lectures from my teachers for not having done my homework. I plowed through the assignments crossly while everyone else was at recess and during lunch, managed to turn in the finished papers before the school day ended, and felt almost cheerful as the bus dropped me off at the farm gates.

Humming under my breath, I got the mail from the mailbox and sorted through it as I walked toward the barn. There were a few dull-looking letters, addressed directly to the farm, and two of my favorite horse magazines.

"Hi, I'm home," I called out as I went through the open stable doors.

Cam's voice answered from one of the stalls beyond the office. "Welcome. Have a good day at school? I'm just about done giving the twin foal her bottle. I'll be right out."

I went into the office, tossed the mail onto the desk, and sat down on the couch in front of the window to flip through one of the magazines. Sunlight poured through the window behind me. Rows of framed photographs looked down from the walls, pictures taken of Mom and Dad smiling together in the winner's circle when one or another of our horses had won an important race. I didn't need to see their faces clearly. I knew the pictures by heart.

CHAPTER

Nine

Cam came in a few minutes later, looking fresh and happy. "The little twin's just fine. Everything's under control."

She picked up the mail and started to open it. "I think we can let the foals go out with their mommas in the small paddocks close to the stable for an hour or so this afternoon. It was too cold and windy this morning. . . ."

Her voice trailed off with a little choking sound. I

looked up quickly. Her face was chalky white. Even her lips had lost their color.

"It's from the bank," she said in a low voice. "This letter. They're going to foreclose on the mortgage. Dad let several payments go by, and we've never been able to catch up. They're going to take our farm away."

"But they can't do that," I said in a perfectly reasonable voice. "We'll get straightened out. We just need a little more time. We're going to lease some of the back land out next summer, and we'll hay our own fields for next winter—" I didn't mention what we both knew so well, that we'd have enough hay from our own land because we had so few horses left. "And we'll have more foals next year, and the year after that we can send them to the sales—and there's Glory Now. Maybe we could sell him to somebody who doesn't know any better—after all, he's undefeated in his racing career. Sounds good, as long as we don't mention the fact he only ran once, and what a crummy bunch of horses he beat—" I was babbling, and I knew it. I shut up.

"They're going to take the horses, too," Cam said.

There was a long and terrible silence. Cam finally turned to the other two envelopes on the desk and opened them slowly, bracing herself for more dreadful news. But the first was from a company recommending that we buy a brand-new twelve-horse air-conditioned van at a tremendous price, painted, at no extra charge, in our very own stable colors. The second one suggested that our stable manager needed a private plane to simplify his busy schedule.

Cam and I both managed stiff shared smiles over these expensive toys before she threw the letters away and picked up the one from the bank again. "I think I should go down to the bank right away," she said at last. "I'll go see Mr. Brewster there. He was a long-time friend of Dad's."

"Good idea," I said brightly. There had to have been some kind of mistake. Certainly the bank must know that breeding good racehorses took time. Surely Mr. Brewster had to have known Dad hadn't been well, but that Cam and I were perfectly capable of pulling the farm back together and making it successful again—

Cam went off in her small white car and I went to turn out the mares and foals.

I started with dear, quiet Pamela and her strong bay colt. She knew the routine perfectly. She waited patiently while I put on her halter and a lead rope, then called softly to her colt and walked out into the sunshine. The colt bounced along beside her like a Ping-Pong ball, but stayed obediently close by her side.

It was always a relief, though, to see them safely behind the white boards of the paddock fence with the gate shut firmly and latched. Foals were skittery little things, right from the beginning, and usually two people took out each mare and foal in case the youngster ran off in the wrong direction by accident and the mare got hysterical.

The chocolate brown mare went out next with her colt, and the colt wandered away just once. The mare let out a yell I'm sure could have been heard in the next county, the colt whisked around and dashed back to her, and I practically shoved them both through the gate of the nearest paddock. I'd wait for Cam before I even tried to bring them in.

I went to get the Secretariat mare next, but I lost my nerve at the last minute. Getting everything together and keeping it together was tough enough with one mare and one foal—who knew what would happen if the twins split in two different directions at the same time? Would the young mare panic?

I decided that even if she didn't panic, I would. I opened the top of the outside door of their stall to the sunshine and decided to leave well enough alone. The foaling stalls were huge, and the fillies were jumping around like little kangaroos. There was plenty of room for them to play in their stall, at least for today.

I went to watch over the colts and mares. Pamela had more sense than to race around with her new baby and half run him to death, as some mares would do their first time out after foaling, but I didn't know the chocolate mare well enough to be sure how she'd behave. She was certainly uneasy at first and paced along her paddock fence for a short while, with her colt bobbing along beside her like a little cork on a fishing line, but the mare soon settled down and began to nibble at the short wintery grass.

I sat down on the ground, folded my arms around my knees, and watched the two colts discover how to trot and gallop in the new freedom of their paddocks. I loved to watch foals playing, but my mind wandered back to Cam, wondering what she'd find out from Mr. Brewster at the bank.

She was home very soon. Too soon. I knew somehow the news was bad, and I was right. Dad's dear friend at the bank, who'd been delighted to come to all our parties in the past and be a guest in our box at the races, had been cold and uncaring. There was no more time. The bank wanted the overdue payments on the mortgage, or the farm must go.

Mr. Brewster was terribly sorry, he'd said, but the bank had its duties and obligations. Good-by, Camilla, how nice it was to see you. Do stop in again some time.

Cam and I looked at each other, stunned.

"Do you mean everything's over, really over, and there's nothing we can do?" I said finally.

Cam just nodded. "I wish I could talk to Jimmy," she said. "He should know the farm's horses he has in training won't belong to us much longer. I don't know what happens about training fees—anyway, I'd just like to talk to him for a little while. I think I'll see if the home farm knows where he is."

She drove off again and I looked around me at the fields and woods I'd always known and cared so much about. And all the horses—but I couldn't bear to think about them, not right now. Where would we go? What was going to happen to us? Maybe Cam had better marry Cliff, after all. . . .

It was a scary feeling and all more than I could handle right away. I shut out every thought I could. I dragged through school in the next string of days and did the chores in the stable and didn't ask another question. I knew Cam went to at least two more banks, hoping for help, but it was useless. There were too many numbers involved and far too many legal words I couldn't understand. Our part-time help had turned into no help at all and never showed up again. Cam and I ate frozen dinners when we remembered to put them in the oven, and apples and carrots when we didn't.

My friend Lyn called one Friday afternoon while I was in the office, just about to start giving the horses their evening feed.

"Hi, stranger," she said. "I tried to catch up with you after the last class this afternoon, but you'd already split for the bus."

"I'm sorry," I said, "but I'm always so worried I'll miss it—Cam can't leave the horses until I get back. What's up?"

"We're having a class meeting on Saturday afternoon. I wanted to make sure you knew about it. Everybody's coming. It'll be more like a party, really. I was hoping you'd be able to be there. We'd get to see something of you for a change, outside of classes."

"I wish I could," I said. "But there's no way. We've got three outside mares coming in to Rondelay, and the van'll be bringing them some time Saturday. I can't leave Cam to deal with all that by herself."

Lyn sighed. "Of course not," she said. "That's tough. Tell me, Steph, how long are you going to try to keep up with all you're doing now?"

I hesitated. I didn't want to talk about the farm coming to an end, not now, not even with my best friend. "We'll play it just one day at a time," I said. "Things will work out."

"Sure," Lyn said. "Everybody'll miss you on Saturday, but that's the way it is—"

We talked for a while, but I could hear the horses beginning to fuss in their stalls as they waited for their

69

evening grain. One or two were kicking at the stall partitions impatiently.

"I've got to go, Lyn," I said. "The horses won't wait. Call me again, will you? And I'll see you on Monday—"

We said good-by. It was hard to remember when there'd last been time for such things as class meetings on weekends. . . . I snatched my jacket from the back of the office chair and hurried to the horses.

The weaker twin filly grew stronger and brighter every day. She no longer needed a bottle every hour. We changed her schedule to every two hours, and then every four, which gave Cam and me more time to sleep at night, though I'm not sure Cam slept much, anyway.

There were funny, happy moments, like getting the mare and her twins out to their paddock on sunny, warm afternoons. If one filly didn't spin and race around its mother, driving her into a frenzy, the other one did. But Cam and I together managed reasonably well, and it was a delight to watch the two little ones scamper around the paddock together. I could lean on the fence and watch them for hours at a time, blanking out everything else around me, and I did this as often as I could.

Ten

I kept busy every minute. I taught the new foals to wear their tiny foal halters, and this helped to keep everything more under control when Cam and I led the mares and foals outside. I scrubbed out feed tubs and water buckets and aired them in the sun, and brushed and groomed every horse I could handle. I swept the stable aisle until the broom nearly wore out, dusted the unused tack in the tack room, and did all the thousands of little things always waiting to be done in a stable. Most of all, I tried not to think.

I managed pretty well for a while. I was almost proud of myself until the big white sign was put up at the farm gates, telling the world the farm had failed and would be put up for auction.

Then the men came, gray-faced men, driving a long, dark car and wearing dark suits. I didn't know what they'd come for. I heard the car and went to the stable door. They were from the bank, they told me eventually, come to look over the house and the stables and land.

"Certainly you must have been notified we were coming today," one of them said. I just shrugged my shoulders. I hadn't known, but I couldn't see that it mattered. They were here, as they would have been, anyway, whether I'd been expecting them or not.

The men all looked alike to me, and I didn't even know which one had spoken. I put the broom away wordlessly and waited to be told what they wanted me to do.

The gray men huddled together. I knew finally what they reminded me of—pictures I'd seen on television of vultures waiting to devour dead things.

Though they had a map of the property, I had to show them some of the closed stables. I offered to show them the big back pastures where the broodmares were, but they looked at the rutted path streaked with wintery ice and mud, and clearly were more concerned about getting their shiny shoes dirty than about the pasture land.

"That's enough for today, I think," said the man with the notebook. "The surveyors will update anything we've missed." They didn't even stop to admire the pretty golden twins in the first stall. They'd be in touch with Cam, they said, who was of legal age and therefore more believable than I was, I supposed.

I leaned numbly against the stable door as I watched the car drive away. It had gotten colder. Clouds were banking up to the west. I hoped fiercely it would snow and the unpleasant men would have a rotten trip back to wherever they'd come from.

"I'm so sorry." Cam held me in her arms when she got back later that afternoon. "I didn't know they were coming today or I'd have given you some warning. It must have been terrible for you."

I could only nod a little.

The appraisers from a livestock agency came to look at the horses two days later. I knew about them, this time, but they were supposed to come in the morning, while I was in school. No such luck.

73

They had been delayed. They apologized. I shrugged my shoulders—who cared why they were late?—and started to show them the horses.

They were only there to see the Thunder Rock Farm horses, but they stopped to admire the sparkling twin fillies and their lovely golden mother. They were real horsemen and they clearly liked several of the horses, especially Rondelay, the yearling by Sir Ivor, and Pamela and her new colt. I felt proud of our stock, but I felt, at the same time, that I was betraying them as I opened each stall door.

I led out each horse while the men talked bloodlines and ruffled through pages of their notebooks. There was a bitter wind blowing, but they were wearing sheepskin coats and boots and didn't mind going down the lane to the broodmare pasture after they'd seen all the horses in the stable.

I'd taken out a measure of oats, so the mares were easy to catch. Each of the broodmares was supposed to wear a leather halter with her name and that of her sire and dam on a narrow brass plate fastened to the halter cheek-piece, though, like horses everywhere, they usually lost them in the pasture.

But there were no problems. Some of the mares had been raced and so had tattoo numbers on their upper lips. All of them had distinguishing markings and were

74

quickly identified. They matched up with the names and pedigrees on the Thunder Rock list, and we hurried back to the stable to get out of the wind.

We stood inside the doors; I didn't invite them into the office. I'd had more than enough and I wanted them to go.

"There seems to be one horse missing."

I stared at the man blankly.

"There are the two-year-olds in training, but they're down in Florida. You know about them. You mentioned them earlier," I said at last.

"Not the two-year-olds," the other man said. "There's a gray mare listed here. Roses Red. Bold Ruler on her sire's side, dam of the Mahmoud line—"

"Rosie." I turned to look at Rosie's empty stall. I wondered hazily if I was going to be sick. I hadn't been able to imagine Rosie belonging to anyone else in the world and so I'd refused to think about it at all. Rosie was more than just another horse. She was mine, and Cam's, and she was so many happy yesterdays with Mom and Dad, and the good times we'd had.

It was all too much. I wished I could cry, but I was beyond tears. On stiff, numb legs I walked slowly over to the stall door and rubbed the brass plate beside it with the sleeve of my jacket.

I wished then that Cam or I had made ourselves stop

to think more about Rosie. Because if we had, we'd have remembered. I stood looking at her nameplate with blurry eyes.

"You can't have Rosie," I said. "She doesn't belong to the farm. She belongs to my sister and to me."

I looked into the dim, empty stall, but I could see Rosie there, popping her lips and waggling her long gray ears. At the same time, I thought of one special Christmas, and could see the sweet, clean snow falling and hear the bells around Rosie's neck ringing as Cam and I rode her together, bareback, while Mom and Dad watched from the window. The morning they'd given Rosie to us for our own. It seemed like a different time in a different world—

"She's registered in our names," I said carefully and very slowly. "Not in the name of Thunder Rock. You can check with the Jockey Club if you don't believe me. The list you have is wrong."

The men were frowning as I turned to face them. "She's a very well-bred mare," one of them said, going through his papers again.

"I know that," I said patiently.

"A valuable mare," the other man said.

"It doesn't change a thing." I wanted to laugh, I wanted to shout, but my voice shook only a little bit. "Rosie doesn't go with the other horses. She doesn't belong to the farm. She was given to my sister and me for Christmas. Several years ago. The transfer papers would be in the file."

One of the men smiled. "I hope you're right, young lady," he said. "We'll have to check it out, of course, but I sure hope you're right. It's hard enough to lose all this—it would be nice to have one good mare left to keep." He reached out to shake my hand. "Good luck," he said.

Cam was late getting home. As soon as she'd changed into jeans, we brought the horses in, and we were too busy to talk while we were feeding them and settling them down for the night.

"I have something to tell you," I said at last.

"Okay." Cam followed me into the warm office, took off her jacket, and waited.

"The men came from the livestock agency to see the horses," I said.

"Yes. I'm sorry. All these worst things seem to get put on your shoulders. It isn't fair to you—"

"I'm all right," I said. "It isn't any worse for me than it is for you. Anyway, neither of us has been very smart. We've been too worried, I guess, and too busy, and too scared—it doesn't matter. You'd better find a pretty big apartment when we have to move out of here. Because Rosie's coming, too."

Cam looked up at me thoughtfully. "You know you're

out of your mind," she said calmly. "What are you planning to do? Steal her and hide her under your bed? I don't think the bank would care much for that."

"Mr. Brewster and his treasured bank can stuff it," I said, just as calmly. "We always felt all the horses on the place were ours, just as Thunder Rock was ours. They're not. Not anymore. But you've forgotten, just as I did. Rosie's not registered in the name of the farm."

"Christmas," Cam whispered, remembering.

"Exactly," I said.

Eleven

Cam sat in silence for a little while. "You're right," she said at last. "You're absolutely right. Oh, Stephany, you're wonderful. What sensational news. One horse of our own, and to think it's Rosie. I suppose it's silly, isn't it, how much it helps? I wonder where we can keep her— but we'll find a way. Rosie is ours, and that's all that matters."

In a glow of shared delight, we put the feed cart away and tidied the stable aisle.

"Guess who's back from Florida?" Cam said at last. "Jimmy—he just got in. He called me at the office. He has to leave again in a few days, but he's going to take us both out to dinner tonight. We can celebrate Rosie."

Beautiful. We showered and changed. It was great to see Jimmy's broad smile again, and the way his tanned, strong hands held Cam's jacket for her as though she was a warm, precious person, not the fragile doll Cliff seemed to see. Great to drive with him to our favorite neighborhood restaurant, where we hadn't been for ages and where everyone seemed glad to see us. We were given one of the very best tables, a lot of people smiled and came by to say hello, and someone—we never were able to find out who it was—sent over a bottle of champagne with a note: "We're all so sorry about what you're going through, but remember this—even bad luck can't last forever."

Jimmy raised his glass to Cam. She raised hers in turn with a smile I'd never seen her give Cliff—or anyone else I could think of, for that matter. I watched in happy silence. It was a wonderful evening.

I thanked Jimmy and said good night as soon as we got home, then went straight to bed, leaving Cam and Jimmy in the kitchen together making coffee and talking. It was a friendly, warm sound. I drifted off into a dreamless sleep for the first time in months.

"Did you ask Jimmy about Rosie?" I asked Cam the next morning. "Is she okay? When's he going to bring her back?"

Cam gave me a glass of fresh orange juice.

"She'll be home tomorrow or the next day. He says she's fine, but he wouldn't tell me anything more," she said. "He said the rest is a secret and he doesn't want to tell us yet."

"That's a funny thing to say," I said uneasily. "You're sure nothing's happened to her?"

"I'm sure. He promised." Cam was making pancakes and turning them with a happy twist of her wrist. After the way I'd stuffed myself silly the night before at dinner, I hadn't thought I'd be hungry again for a week. But the pancakes tasted marvelous, golden in the middle and crisp around the edges, just as I liked them best.

"I don't think I'll be able to bend over all day," I said. "No more, thanks, Cam. I'm stuffed. And I've got to catch the school bus."

Cam glanced at her watch. "Golly, you're right. You'd better be on your way. I hope you have a reasonably pleasant day today."

Later that afternoon, after Cam had come home, we brought all the horses into the stable. I pushed the feed cart down the aisle, heaping the measures with sweet golden oats and mixed feed, loving the warm, friendly

81

sound of horses munching contently as I moved from stall to stall. We'd hung a second feed tub in each of the big foaling stalls, and I poured a little scattering of grain in each of them. This gave the young foals a chance to practice nibbling on the grain, rolling it around in their tiny mouths and getting used to the new taste and texture. Some mares would let their foals share the grain in their own feed tubs, but not all of them would permit such a thing. The two colts already had teeth but weren't sure yet what they were for. By starting them early, when they were old enough to understand grain and how to eat it, they'd be ready and demand less milk from their mothers.

I gave the twin fillies a handful of crushed oats in their feed tub. They weren't as far along as the colts, and crushed oats were more an interesting new toy to them than real food.

The stronger filly no longer shoved her little sister away, because little sister had grown stronger and had learned how to shove back. The smaller filly was nursing often, demanding her turn. The mother had milk enough for both, and though we continued to offer the smaller twin a bottle of formula several times each day, she was losing interest, which meant she was getting her share from her mother.

I watched the two of them jostling each other and then turning together to play in the stall while their mother polished the last of her dinner from the bottom of her feed tub. Even Dr. Bailey, who must have seen a thousand foals, liked to stop by several times a week to see the twins. Cam began to worry about the stable call bills, but one day the doctor explained he wasn't counting these as stable calls—he just plain enjoyed watching the twins. He said we had good reason to be pleased with how well we'd done in raising them.

Cam went off for an appointment one Saturday and came home in the afternoon looking furious. "I'm tired of strangers running our lives and telling us what to do," she said. "And they sure don't care. Bankers. Lawyers—"

"I guess you heard from another dear old friend," I said with a sudden flash of understanding. "Who was it this time?"

"Bill Pawling," Cam answered. "Our trusted, friendly family attorney. You remember him, don't you? He used to love to come here to the parties before the yearling sales. And he and his wife both always had a little too much eggnog at our New Year's parties. He always brought Mom huge bunches of white roses."

I nodded. I remembered Mr. Pawling and his stiff wads of roses, which Mom would stuff into the old chipped lemonade pitcher in the kitchen after thanking the Pawlings politely for their thoughtfulness.

"Well, now suddenly the farm hasn't got any money,

the banks are screaming, we have no clout, and Mom and Dad's dear friend Bill has lost interest. The appointment with him today was to try to get some of this mess straightened out. He took me to the Lime Tree for lunch and the bill would have run this place for a week. He kept patting me every chance he got, and when I told him politely to get lost, he wasn't pleased. Not at all."

Cam shivered. "There's so much big money in Thoroughbreds suddenly, all out of proportion. . . . It makes you wonder a little, doesn't it, Steph? Outside pressures— I don't know. Maybe somebody wants our farm or our horses that badly— First thing, I'm going to try to find a new lawyer. Someone on *our* side, for a change. But I think it's too late to save Thunder Rock."

Jimmy couldn't have come at a better time. We were giving the horses their evening feed when suddenly he appeared at the stable door. Cam fell into his arms like a drowning swimmer who'd suddenly found a life raft. I busied myself with the horses while they went into the office to talk.

Jimmy came down the stable aisle with Cam to see the horses, as he always did. He enjoyed watching the twins, but his eyes gleamed when he saw Pamela's colt. "Sired by your Rondelay, isn't he?" he asked Cam. "And that's your Princequillo mare, right? Classic lines. This young fellow should be able to run a little, come time."

84

Cam nodded in agreement. "I don't know why Dad didn't plan more Rondelay foals," she said. "I practically sneaked this mare to Rondelay last spring, and she was in foal before Dad knew a thing about it. He was sending our mares everywhere to all kinds of second-rate stallions the owners somehow persuaded him were good horses, just because they paid too much money for them."

"Yes, I know," said Jimmy. "It never made much sense to me, either. We had a few talks about it, but he didn't want to listen to what I had to say. He was so lost and lonely after your mother died, and so ready to listen to people who didn't know a scrap of what he knew. They were running pedigrees through their new computers and telling your dad the old days were done, that computer planning of breeding programs was the only way to go. So he spent a fortune on shipping fees and stud fees and mare care at all kinds of places, just to keep his new friends happy—at least, he thought they were friends. When all they wanted were his money and his first-class mares. And look what happened."

"Junk is what happened," I said over my shoulder. "Good mares wasted producing useless foals that grew up to be like that no-good Glory Now."

"And a sheriff's notice at the gates," added Cam. "Poor Dad. It certainly doesn't take long for a respected breeding farm to lose its good name. I know you need a little luck to breed a quality yearling or winning racehorse, never mind what the computers say, but basic common sense doesn't hurt any."

"What about the other mares, the ones you told me he never remembered to send out last year?" asked Jimmy.

"They're in great shape," I said. "We keep them mostly out in the back pasture with the big shed there for shelter. We give them grain and hay, of course. But I guess if horses wonder at all, they must be wondering what's happened to them."

"Poor Dad," Cam said again. "Charmed by a bunch of rip-off artists into a poor breeding program when there was no one who was better at planning good bloodlines than he was, when things were right. . . ."

"Where's Rosie?" I finally had the chance to say. "Is she all right? When's she coming back?"

"She's fine. I'll have her back here tomorrow."

We went into the house. Cam found some hamburger at the back of the freezer, I found a jar of tomato sauce and a box of spaghetti, and while we put a big pot of water on to boil, Jimmy made a salad, mostly from the carrots we always had in the refrigerator for the horses.

We didn't talk about our farm or our problems all through supper. Sitting around the round white kitchen table, we ate spaghetti and laughed at the stories Jimmy told us about his young racing string and some of the new owners and their impossible demands.

It wasn't until all the dishes were stacked in the sink and coffee had been made that Jimmy asked more about the farm.

"What a miserable business," he said when we'd finished. "I've heard some talk. Here and there. It's impossible to track down the sources. There's some very big money waiting out there—I don't know either, Cam. I'd hoped the bank might at least give you an extension."

"I tried, as you know," said Cam. "But no way."

There was a silence. "I think the saddest part of all," she said in a low voice, "is the way Thunder Rock will go out so defeated and so forgotten. After all the splendid horses we've raised and raced in the past."

I started to do the dishes. Cam and Jimmy went on talking. I left the dishes to drain dry and went out to the barn. I didn't want to hear any more.

CHAPTER

Twelve

Jimmy brought Rosie home the next afternoon. I'd already swept out her stall right across from the office, put down huge amounts of fresh bedding, and had everything clean and bright and waiting as soon after school as I could manage.

It was so good to have her back. She looked marvelous; Jimmy would have made sure of that. I took the shipping wraps off her legs and groomed her for an hour, treasuring the wonderful feeling of having her home again.

"You'll brush every hair out of her tail if you don't stop fussing over this mare," Cam said with a laugh, when she came to tell me it was time for us to bring in the horses from the outside paddocks for the night.

But I saw her sneak into the stall and give Rosie a huge hug before we started the evening work.

"Jimmy's asked us both out to dinner with him tonight," Cam said later.

"That's great," I said, "but I've got an awful lot of homework to do. You two go ahead. I'll be fine."

I didn't want to be tagging along with Jimmy and Cam every minute. Cliff had called just the evening before to talk to Cam, but he was somewhere a long way away. I wasn't sure where, but I didn't care, as long as he was there and Jimmy was here. Tough for Cliff, I thought to myself joyfully as I watched Cam and Jimmy drive off.

I put a huge pile of hay in the corner of Rosie's stall and curled up in it to catch up on two chapters in my history book. The light was on in Rosie's stall so I could read, though all the other stalls were in darkness and the horses were quiet. Rosie thumped her feed tub as she often did, hoping it would somehow produce another measure of grain. The empty rubber tub bounced lightly against the oak wall, and the fasteners rattled with a cheerful sound.

"You know that never works, you greedy thing," I said to the mare fondly. "You've had all the grain for today you're going to get."

I pulled an apple from my pocket, took one bite, and gave the rest to Rosie. I snuggled further down in the hay, feeling happy and peaceful for the first time in ages, while Rosie finished her apple and started nibbling at the hay around me.

The light flickered in the stall. I glanced up at the bulb impatiently. It was always such a production to change a light bulb in a stall, taking the horse out, tying it up safely out of the way, carrying the clumsy ladder down the aisle and into the stall—I hoped the bulb would last just a little while longer. And then I heard the terrible shriek of the smoke alarm at the far end of the stable.

I froze. My heart was jumping and thumping with fear, and I couldn't move a single part of me. But this only lasted a second or two— The horses. I must get the horses out— But maybe the alarm was only signaling that it needed a new battery, though Cam and I replaced each battery every six months.

I went to Rosie's stall door. The harsh cries of the alarm made me shiver. It was a dreadful high, thin sound, like invisible shards of glass flying through the dark stable, cutting right into me. Just in case the alarm wasn't faking, I took Rosie's halter quietly from its place outside her door, clipped on the lead rope, and put the halter on her head. I whacked the outdoor floodlight switches beside the main door of the stable to turn them all on and led Rosie out into the night. She seemed a little puzzled to be shut in one of the small nearby paddocks at this hour, but it seemed a wise thing to do, even though I still wasn't sure whether or not the screaming smoke alarm meant anything at all.

With Rosie's paddock gate safely latched, I raced back to the barn, and this time I smelled smoke. A second alarm, with a different, wavering scream, started an ugly duet with the first.

I knew I should call the fire department—I knew I should get the horses out. . . . Paralyzed with indecision, I stood just inside the stable door.

Horses first. If I knew anything at all about stable fires, it was how quickly horses died in them—I'd get to the horses first.

The young Secretariat mare was moving restlessly in her stall, bumping into her bewildered twins. But she let me put her halter on, and the twins, terrified by the screeching alarms, stayed close beside her. I led her at a trot into the paddock next to Rosie's.

The chocolate mare wouldn't let me touch her. A third alarm had joined the first two, the smell of smoke was getting stronger, and she was half out of her mind with fear. I opened her stall door that led to the outside, shouted at her to run, and forced myself to leave her to go on to the next stall.

Pamela was nervous and nickering constantly to her colt, who was jumping in little circles in fright. No time to put on her halter—I yanked the belt from my jacket, put it around her neck, and led her outside. The foal lost track of his mother for a few terrifying moments, but she whinnied loudly and he flew to her side. I slammed and latched their paddock gate and ran back to the barn again.

There were flames now, creeping from the windows of the big tack room at the far end of the stable.

I dove into the office and grabbed the phone. The emergency number of the local fire department was written in huge numbers on a notice taped to the wall, but I was so wild with fright I couldn't dial. I called the operator instead.

"There's a stable fire at the Reed Farm," I said the very second she answered. "Thunder Rock. Quick, report it to the fire department—"

"You may call the department directly," she said. "The number is—"

"Tell them the stable is burning," I said, and threw the receiver to the floor. I heard the operator's voice squeaking that someone should be at the mailbox to guide the fire engines. "I'm alone. They'll see the flames," I shouted at the fallen phone, and ran to the horses.

The Sir Ivor yearling let me catch him and I got him safely to a paddock. The others were so frightened they wouldn't let me anywhere near them. Glory came at me with his teeth bared in terror and striking out with his forehoofs. I dodged out of his way, flung open his outside door to give him every possible chance to escape, and tore to Rondelay's stall.

The old stallion was standing in the center of his stall, motionless with fear, sweating and shaking all over. I put his halter on, but he wouldn't move a step. I yanked off my jacket, wrapped it around his head, and somehow managed to get him outside. He made a sudden dive away from me, trying to get back to the stall, which had always been his place of refuge and shelter.

He couldn't understand the danger. Grimly I hung onto him and led him to the gateway of the lane to the back pasture. The gate sagged and was heavy, but I yanked at it with a strength I didn't know I had, pulled my jacket off the stallion's head, and hit him with it on his hindquarters as hard as I could. He shied away from it and raced away from me, down the lane. Even above the alarms and the whinnies of the frightened horses still in the stable, I could hear the neighing of the broodmares as he galloped toward their pasture. With a choking sob of relief, I shoved the gate shut so he couldn't try to dash back to his stall again. Then all the lights went out—

the outside floodlights as well as those inside the stable.

There was no moon. In the miserable dark, I stumbled down the outside of the stable, sliding back all the bolts I could find. I couldn't remember which stalls held horses and which were empty, but there was no time to try to remember. It made no difference. All I could do was open every door to give the horses the chance to save themselves if they could. Or would.

Then there was light again, but this time from the flames shooting suddenly through the roof of the tack room. I could hear the terrified mares running with their foals in the nearby paddocks, and the crashing sound of galloping hoofs as some of the horses ran free from the smoky, terrifying confinement of their stalls.

There was nothing, absolutely nothing in the world, more that I could do. I stayed out by the small paddocks, trying to calm the frightened mares there with my voice. I could just see the dim, gray shape of Rosie back at the very end of her paddock, pressed against the board fence, as far away from the fire as she could get. In the ugly orange light of the flames, I could see the Secretariat mare galloping. I hoped she wouldn't run herself into the fence and break her neck in her fear, or trample her foals, though I was powerless to stop her. Pamela was trotting uneasily in her paddock, but she kept her colt close by her flank. I couldn't see any of the others.

I heard the wailing sirens of the fire engines at last. I'd never heard a more glorious sound. I couldn't tell how much time had gone by. It might have been minutes or hours—I had no way of knowing.

I couldn't move as they came roaring into the stable drive. There was nothing to tell anybody, anyway. For sure, they didn't need me to show them where the fire was. The night dark was stabbed with strange new colors mixing with the streaky orange and yellow flames. Sharp red and blue and white lights flashed as police cars came, followed by more fire engines. Nobody shouted. I heard short commands, the mechanical pulsing sound of the powerful engines, the quick footsteps of the fire fighters in their heavy boots, and then, at last, the hiss of water pouring onto the spreading flames while another truck turned its hoses on the roof of the house to protect it.

I never saw Cam until I felt her arms around me. "You're all right, you're all right," she said, over and over again.

"I'm all right," I repeated stupidly, my voice hoarse with smoke and fear.

We stood in silence. I could feel Cam shaking. I wasn't shaking. I guessed hazily that I was beyond reacting anymore in any way. Gratefully, I was aware that I was mostly stunned now and numb.

We stood together and watched the crazily jumping

flames and the sparks they shot into the air. At some time, Jimmy found us and stayed with us, holding both of us close.

"There's nothing I can do to help," he said to Cam. "I thought it would be best just to stay out of the way and try to find the two of you."

Cam just nodded.

The terrible noise of the flames began to fade. Voices of individual fire fighters called once in a while, though we couldn't always make out what they were saying. The rush of the water from the fire hoses became louder than the sounds of the fire itself.

"I think they're getting it under control," said Jimmy. "It looks as though the worst is over."

CHAPTER

Thirteen

We stayed where we were. There was still an awful lot of smoke pouring out everywhere, moving like creepy ghosts through the fierce bright floodlights of the fire engines.

We heard one fire fighter say to another, "How many horses were in here? Were any of them gotten out?"

I'd told Cam about the few I'd been able to lead to safety. Even I couldn't have told him how many of the others had run free. I didn't know for sure. I'd done what I could.

"We'll find out in the morning," another man said. "Should be daylight pretty soon."

I blinked my sore eyes toward the eastern horizon. There were pale streaks of light behind the trees. Objects gradually began to take shape. The silhouettes of the huge fire engines, the police cars, and even the pasture fencing were beginning to show a little in blurry outline.

I forced myself to turn around. Rosie was still pressed motionlessly against the paddock fence. I hardly dared look at the paddock with the chestnut mare and her twins—she'd been so terribly frightened—but at last I was able to make out three shapes, the one mare and both the little blobs of shadow with white markings, which were her foals.

Only full daylight would let us see if they'd been hurt, or where any of the other horses were. Pamela and her colt were too dark to distinguish in the dim light. I could only hope for the best, and I wasn't sure I dared hope anything at all.

Stiffly, as though we were windup mechanical dolls, we went into the kitchen of the house and started to make coffee for the fire fighters. Jimmy carried mugs and cups out to them while Cam and I boiled water and made more. We carefully avoided looking out of the windows as the daylight grew stronger.

After his fifth trip, Jimmy sat down on a kitchen stool. "The chief will be in to see you in a few minutes," he told Cam.

With my back to Jimmy, I asked the question that had to be asked by someone. "Have they been able to go through the stable yet?" I said.

"They're doing it now," said Jimmy. "The fire is out and the smoke is clearing."

"I should go out there," said Cam in a muffled voice.

Jimmy put out a restraining hand. "Not yet. Wait just a little bit more. Then we'll all go together."

The huge form of the fire chief appeared at the kitchen door. "Miss Camilla, ma'am?" he said to Cam. We all looked at him in silence. "May I come in?"

"Oh, I'm so sorry, of course." Cam poured a fresh mug of coffee, which the chief accepted with courtesy, though he didn't drink it.

"We can't be sure yet what started the fire," the chief said. "We've just finished checking the main stable. We found four horses there, ma'am. But if it's any comfort, it looked as though the fire itself never reached them. Probably they died from the smoke. Happens with horses in these stable fires, more times than not."

Numbly, we followed him outside. Soft sunshine was

pouring through the early morning mist and mixing with the last of the smoke from the fire. "We'll leave an engine here with a crew for a while longer," said the chief. "We don't want to risk the fire starting up again. They'll keep an eye on things until we're sure it's safe. Most of the main building's untouched, did you know that?"

I heard Cam murmuring her thank-you's and her gratitude. The police cars were gone and most of the fire engines left a few minutes later.

I turned with hesitant footsteps toward the paddocks. It was time to find out what damage had been done to the few horses I'd tried to keep safe in their small paddocks, before the fire and smoke had made anything more impossible to do.

We went first to the mares and foals. Rosie, still frightened, wouldn't even touch the apple I offered her, but she seemed not to have been hurt, as far as we could tell. Jimmy, Cam, and I went next to the Secretariat mare and her twins. I kept my eyes on the ground. I couldn't bear to look.

"There's only a little cut on one of the twins," said Jimmy, coming back to me. "And a bruise on the other, but just on the ribs, and I don't think they're broken. No other damage done that we can find."

I followed them to Pamela's paddock but still couldn't really look. My eyes didn't lift from the ashy grass until both Cam and Jimmy came to tell me they seemed all right, too.

"You did an incredible job with those mares," said Jimmy.

"I couldn't get the chocolate mare to leave her stall," I said, shaking my head. I didn't want anybody telling me how wonderful I was when I didn't feel that way at all. My voice sounded a long way away. "I'm going to look for Rondelay. I chased him down the lane toward the broodmare pasture. But I heard fencing breaking. Maybe he got hurt."

I knew Cam or Jimmy was about to offer to go with me, but suddenly I didn't want to be with anyone. I wanted to get away by myself, just for a little while, and away from the terrible smell of smoke and the dead horses I knew were in the stable, lying in what they'd always known as the peaceful protection of their stalls. What more should I have done?

I started to run unevenly toward the back lane. I wiggled through the bars of the gate and tried to go on running toward the far pasture, but I had to slow to a walk. My throat was sore from all the smoke, and I could only breathe in shuddering gasps.

At least I could smell the morning here a little. I could hear birds singing as though nothing awful had ever happened. I saw the delicate white and green pattern of snowdrops flowering in sunny, sheltered places, and I saw a rabbit watching me from under a bush at the side of the lane. He hopped away slowly, stopping to nibble now and then at a grass tip he considered special. He wasn't afraid. I watched him for a minute or two. It was nice to look at a living thing that showed no signs of fear, after last night—

I went on. The early rays of the sun sparked tiny rainbows in drops of moisture on the budding leaves of the bushes. The wet grass swished around my ankles and soaked the bottoms of the legs of my jeans. I hardly noticed.

I found the broken fence. The panel next to the pasture gate was in splinters. I stopped to take a rail from another part of the fence and wedged it into the gap. We didn't need the whole band of broodmares and Rondelay rushing through the broken fence down the lane to the stable. Not just now.

I couldn't find any of them at first. I blinked my smarting eyes, puzzled, and then found them at the far side of the rise, down by the edge of the woods, grazing serenely in the morning light. Rondelay was with them, snorting occasionally and pawing the ground, but stopping now and then to do his share of grazing.

I couldn't help a shaky laugh. Raised in the strict formality of a Thoroughbred breeding farm, he'd never had a whole band of mares in a field to himself. He seemed to find it a wonderful idea.

I went down to the mares and shared the few apples I had in my pockets when they came over to me. Rondelay stayed well behind them. Probably he thought I'd come to capture him and take him back to his stall.

"Not right now, fella," I told him. "I just want to make sure you're okay."

He wouldn't let me come near enough to touch him—he didn't want to be caught—but I watched him move, and I could see no more than a scrape on one shoulder, probably from a broken rail. No blood anywhere, and he wasn't limping, so it looked as though he hadn't been hurt.

For the first time in a long time, I felt myself smiling. He looked so proud and free. "Enjoy yourself. All of this is yours for a while," I said.

He watched me go, with his handsome head high and his ears pricked, then trotted back to the scattered mares.

Fourteen

The state police found the chocolate mare and her foal cantering serenely along the highway, more than a mile away, with traffic piling up in both directions. Jimmy called his farm manager and told him to take his van and all the help he could get to catch the wandering mare with her foal and take them back to his place. While I'd been checking Rondelay, Dr. Bailey had come. He and Cam and Jimmy had identified the horses that had died in the fire: two yearlings, one of the mares that had come to be bred to Rondelay, and Glory Now.

When I got back to the barn, I forced myself to glance at one of the yearlings lying dead in his stall. He looked just as though he'd gone peacefully to sleep. I couldn't look at Glory or any of the others. One was enough for me. Glory Now, no matter what his track record was, had been so vital and full of joy and life—I didn't think I could bear to see him lying still forever in his stall.

Dr. Bailey finished examining the dead horses for the necessary official reports. The four of them had been in the stalls nearest the tack room, and they had died from the smoke.

Trucks came to take them away. The fire fighters hosed the hot cinders of what was left of the tack room several times more, and gradually they cooled into piles of wet ashes. Cam finally made me go into the house for a shower. I threw the clothes I'd worn into a pile outside on the porch. They reeked of smoke. So did my hair. I washed it several times and poured lemon rinse on it, trying to get rid of that awful smell. I scrubbed myself until my skin smarted, found an old terry-cloth bathrobe, and wandered vaguely through the house, wondering what to do next. I tried lying down on my bed, and then on Cam's, but I couldn't rest. Each time I closed my eyes, all I could see were smoke and flames, and I heard again

105

the wild, terrible sounds of the alarms and the frightened horses.

Useless. I pulled on fresh clothes and went back outside. There were still too many unanswered questions, anyway— Where were all the other horses that had panicked and run away from the smoke-filled stable?

One by one, reports came in. The horses had scattered all over. Most of them had found their way to different farms nearby and had been taken in. The police, the vets, even the local dog warden had been called, and they all had a pretty good idea where the loose horses had come from. Only one, it turned out, didn't belong to us; a field hunter had jumped out of his pasture to join one of our galloping horses and they'd raced up the driveway of a neighboring farm. One was a little lame, one had a cut on the chest—Dr. Bailey went to see to them. But first he examined the mares and foals on what was left of our own place. He took three stitches in the cut on the twin and said the other mares and foals looked well enough, but that he'd stop by to check them again after he'd seen the others.

He called us from each farm. The lame horse had lost a shoe and chipped his hoof, but fresh shoeing with a pad was probably all he needed. One of our mares did have a cut on her chest, but it wasn't deep and would soon heal. The rest of the horses looked tired but basically all right, and each of the farms said they'd be glad to keep them until we could bring them home.

There was a hushed moment of grateful silence when Cam hung up after the last call. Not one of the horses had been burned.

We were lucky, too, that the day was sunny and mild. The mares and foals would be all right for a while outside in their paddocks.

We were dazed and tired, but things could have been a lot worse. We had a conference at the kitchen table.

"I certainly have room in the farm stable for Rosie," said Jimmy, "for as long as you need a home for her. And I can take in the mare with twins until the owners come to get them, and I can keep Pamela, with her colt, too, of course. No problem. The rest of your broodmares are all right where they are in the pasture—"

"—and so is Rondelay," I said. "I think Dr. Bailey should have a look at him, if we can catch him, but he's perfectly happy where he is for now."

Cam looked up, her face smudged with smoke and all her beautiful hair in tangles, and she laughed—a real, amused laugh. "Bank or no bank, Dad's fancy contracts and computer breeding plans or not, Rondelay's taken over. There's not a single mare out there that isn't Rondelay's now. I said it was a shame Thunder Rock would drift into oblivion because we'd recently had such a rotten breeding program. After last night's adventure, I'd say there are good chances that some especially fine foals will be born next year from this terrible night."

"They won't belong to us, though," I reminded her. "The horses won't be ours."

"We can't help that," Cam said. "Not anymore. But the farm name will be listed as the recorded breeder of each of those foals, however many there might be. By golly, at least the farm will go out with its flag nailed to the mast."

It *was* a nice thought. Little enough to cling to, but a whole lot better than what we'd had, which had been almost nothing at all. Somehow it helped get us all through the rest of that terrible day.

A fire inspector came and practically accused us of setting our own fire because of all our financial problems. "And kill all those horses that meant so much to us?" Cam said, so shocked that even the inspector had to look embarrassed. An insurance man came from the company that covered the barns and buildings, and hinted about the same thing, even going on to propose that I'd been alone in the stable and had probably been smoking in the hay.

"My sister is barely thirteen, doesn't smoke, never has, and the fire started in the tack room, not anywhere where there was hay." Cam was practically snarling by then. "She was in the front stall when the fire started, it was she who first heard the alarms and saved almost all of the horses. If it hadn't been for her—"

The insurance agent crept away to consult with the fire inspector, and a little while later they came to us, looking a little ashamed of themselves, but not nearly enough, to tell us they'd found that the fire started with an electric short, probably in a wire in the tack-room heater. Not the least sign of carelessness, negligence, or arson.

"You were extremely fortunate that there was no hay-loft to spread the fire over the rest of the stable," the insurance man said just before he left.

Cam just smiled politely. Of course there was no loft over our stables. Fire was such a terrible thing in a barn that most breeders built a separate storage building for hay, with concrete walls, if they possibly could, to keep the danger of a hay fire well away from the horses.

Two of the gray men rushed over from the bank and were relieved to see most of the main stable was undamaged. Because the horses that had died were insured, and so the bank's money in them was safe, they hardly mentioned them.

Dr. Bailey came back and Jimmy asked the doctor to check Rosie again, which he was glad to do. I saw them talking in the paddock. Cam and I were so tired by then that everything seemed to be blurry around the edges, but we were glad to see Jimmy show so much concern about Rosie.

We all helped catch Rondelay in the back pasture, which took some doing, but he really was all right. After Dr. Bailey put some ointment on the scrape on the horse's shoulder and patted him, we turned him loose again to go back to his mares, much to Rondelay's surprise and delight.

There were owners of outside horses to be notified, and Jimmy sent his van to collect the mares and foals from our paddocks. Rondelay was old but he wasn't ancient, and he'd be fine sheltering with his new-found mares. But the foals were still too young for it to be good for them to lie down on the cool spring ground for their naps, or to spend long, damp nights outside in the paddocks this early in the year. We certainly didn't want to take any of them back into the main stable, which still smelled awful from all the smoke and was now without either electricity or running water.

Rosie and Pamela with her foal loaded into Jimmy's van without any problems, but the Secretariat mare and the twins were a circus. The fillies danced merrily just out of our reach.

We laughed until we nearly cried. Capturing the bright

little things and getting them up the ramp into the van was like trying to catch fireflies in our bare hands. Finally I managed to hold the mare still; Cam and Jimmy each swooped a golden twin up in their arms, and we got them safely installed in the special big stall ready in the van for them. We ran the ramp up in a rush and shut the big van doors, limp with exhaustion and laughing.

"I sure hope the owners of those little creatures appreciate what they've got," said Jimmy, wiping his eyes. "They're more fun than a month's vacation. I don't think they want the fillies, though. They heard somewhere that no twin ever made a quality racehorse, which is nonsense, but they refuse to believe all the evidence to the contrary. I hear Dr. Bailey's made an offer for the twins."

That was good news. The van moved off slowly so as not to startle the mares or foals. We set out to see our wandering horses and to thank the people who'd been kind enough to take them in.

Every farm and every stable repeated that they'd be glad to take care of the horses until some kind of arrangements could be made for us to have them back.

"Of course, it'll mean they'll be coming back just for the bank sale," I said gloomily as we drove home from the last farm in Jimmy's car.

Cam was determined to find a way to manage. "We'll

open the broodmare barn in the back," she said. "It will only take a day or two to get it cleaned up enough. We'll have the electricity turned on again out there, and the water, and it will do fine. The horses will be here in plenty of time for us to trim them and polish them up and make them look respectable."

I sighed. I was hungry and desperately tired and I didn't want to think about the sale.

We stopped at our favorite McDonald's. Now that we knew where the lost horses were and that they were safe, I suddenly discovered I was starving. I ate everything I'd ordered and most of Cam's french fried potatoes as well as my own, and fell into an exhausted sleep in the back of the car on the way home.

Even the last drifting smell of wet ashes and dead smoke that hung over everything didn't wake me up. Jimmy must have carried me to bed and covered me with a quilt—I didn't remember a thing about it. I slept like a stone.

The next day we were so stiff and tired that everything we did was an unbelievable effort. But Cam and I managed to carry the breeding record files and books from the stable office to the kitchen. The counters and tables were soon deep in papers and ledgers that all smelled sickeningly of smoke, but she plowed through them grimly while I went out with some hay and fresh grain for Rondelay and his mares.

Cliff called. Wherever he was, he'd heard about the fire, and he sounded ready to charter a plane and send for Cam.

"I couldn't leave now, Cliff, honestly. We're coping all right with the horses, but it's all a bit complicated. We're lucky we lost so few."

Cliff wasn't interested in the problems with the horses, and so Cam was able to reassure him. By the time she got done and hung up the phone, she'd managed to make the whole ugly mess sound to Cliff like a picnic in the summer.

"I couldn't get him to understand, so there was no more use trying," Cam said. "He wanted me to go down and join him and his friends on some island or other in the Caribbean—can you imagine? To recover from this, he said, and get away from it all." Cam shook her head wonderingly. "He's really very sweet, but he *can't* understand. . . ." She went back to her columns of depressing figures and I went outside again.

CHAPTER

Fifteen

The two stable cats had vanished during the fire. We had no way of knowing what had happened to them, or even if they'd gotten safely out of the deadly reach of the smoke and fire. I found Milton, the red and white striped tiger with the white paws, sitting cozily in the sun at the stable door at noon, just as though nothing had changed. I fed him and hoped Samantha was all right. By five o'clock that same afternoon, their regular feeding time, Samantha appeared for her dinner. She had singed marks on the crazy patterns of her tortoiseshell coat, but no burns I could find. Both cats seemed puzzled that there were no horses in the main stable, but this didn't stop them from eating a huge amount of supper, then going into the office to curl up on their favorite chair, even though it smelled of smoke, just as though everything were the same as it had always been. I envied them. It must, I decided, be nice to be a cat.

We aired out the broodmare barn, hung clean buckets and feed tubs, and opened its doors and windows to the sunlight. The windows were streaky with dust and there were cobwebs high in the rafters, but when we were done the stalls were safe and snug. One by one, we started to bring the lost horses home.

Mercifully, we were so busy then that the days slipped by in an endless whirl of things to be done. We had to borrow clipping machines and grooming equipment from Jimmy's place. Most of ours had been destroyed in the fire, and it was useless to replace it all. The blacksmith came, and Dr. Bailey, who checked all the horses and told us he had bought the twin fillies.

"I'd heard more than once that their owners were talking of putting them down. I couldn't stop worrying about them. I've got an old mare who'll keep an eye on them, and I'll raise them on substitute formula. They should grow just as well—a lot better than if they were neglected half to death by owners who never wanted them to begin with."

He promised I could go to see them whenever I wanted and drove off with a wave of his hand and a farewell beep of the horn of his mud-spattered unit.

"That's good news, anyway," Cam said. I was too relieved to say much of anything. I tried not to get fond of the outside horses and foals that came and went from the farm, but it wasn't always easy, and the twins were special. We went back to work.

Our work was done. For the first time, Cam sounded as discouraged as I felt as we wandered aimlessly up and down the stable aisle. It was pitch dark and late.

"So many years," she said. "None of them any use at all. Every dream we've ever had is going right down the tubes and we can't even begin to stop any of it from happening. Though goodness only knows how hard we tried."

The next morning was the bank sale. Our dreams and hopes would all belong to the other people who bought our house and the farm and our horses. Nothing left but Cam and me and a single tall, sweet gray mare. It was hard to find any kind of an encouraging tomorrow.

It was harder still to find words to comfort Cam just then. I sure didn't know any.

I was no help to her at all the next morning, either. I took one look at the first truck full of auctioneer's equipment as it turned through the farm gates and thought I'd come apart.

It was going to be a nice day, but the early breeze was cool, so I rolled the heavy doors of the barn closed after the morning feeding, leaving the horses glowing and bright with grooming, rustling their breakfast hay.

The big gray stable doors thundered as they rolled shut, and they met and stopped with a sickening thud full of endings. I knew I'd never be opening them to the morning sun for our horses again. The horses would be gone forever, and so much would be over. My love for them, and my caring, and their sweet, warm presence would have vanished by the end of the day. There'd be nothing but achingly empty stalls as reminders of how much was gone.

I stood with my hands pressed against the doors, feeling a grief so deep I could barely breathe. The sound of those stable doors closing would haunt me forever.

"Go," said Cam, taking one look at my stricken face. "You don't have to stay here to watch. Go for a ride on Rosie and then take her over to Jimmy's. He's expecting her anytime today."

I gave Cam a grateful look and fled. I didn't trust myself to try to speak.

117

There'd been a bridle in the office that had just come back from the saddler with a mended cheekpiece. It hadn't been turned to ashes with all the others in the burned tack room, so I had it to use for Rosie.

She was out in one of the paddocks. I put on the bridle, made sure it was adjusted comfortably for her, and rode away from the barn.

I jogged Rosie down the lane and through the open gate of the broodmare pasture—the mares and Rondelay were all in the stable for the day—jumped her over the rail fence on the far side, and wandered aimlessly through the woods.

It was a perfect Virginia spring morning, sweet with the smell of new buds and warming earth. The Blue Ridge Mountains were violet in the distance. Daffodils danced in sunny clearings and foamy patterns of pink and white trees blossomed in the woods. I wished savagely that it was a gray, miserable day, but I had no more control over the weather than I did over what was happening to our farm and the horses.

Rosie was content to wander quietly along the bridle paths. The sun sailed high overhead and I guessed it must be noon—I'd forgotten to wear my watch, but I couldn't see what difference it could make. I stopped to let Rosie drink from a stream and graze for a while at the ends of the reins. I lay on my back, squinting my eyes against the sun, mindlessly watching tiny puffs of white clouds drift across the uncaring blue of the sky.

The shadows began to lengthen. I knew I couldn't stay out forever. Watch or no watch, I knew it was time to take Rosie to Jimmy's.

One of the grooms told me which was to be Rosie's stall. It had been freshly bedded. I shut her in it and borrowed a brush and went back to work on her coat until it was spotless. I gave her some hay, cleaned her bridle, and wondered what there was left for me to do. I'd been working at Thunder Rock with so many horses for so many months, without a break, that I didn't know how to handle the sudden new freedom. I didn't like it. I stood outside Rosie's door, practically paralyzed with indecision.

The horses were being fed. I knew almost all Jimmy's helpers, and they spoke to me sympathetically, but they had work to do and I felt in the way.

I went outside to sit on a bench near the white stable doors. Window boxes had been freshly planted with scarlet geraniums and dark green ivy. I stared at them fiercely, trying to keep my mind a blank, but I was beginning to feel guilty for leaving Cam without me at the farm. . . .

It was starting to get dark. Lights went on in the stable. The thumps of impatient horses waiting to be fed had stopped, the feed cart had made its last rumbling trip down the aisle. There was the splash of water buckets being topped with fresh water for the night, the rustle of hay— What was I doing here, anyway, sitting in the dim light, with nothing to do but think? I put my face in my hands and wished, as I had a thousand times before, that this whole terrible day had never had to happen.

"It's over." Cam swept me into her car. Jimmy was with her and they sketched in the day for me. Rondelay had gone for a very high price. Pamela and her splendid colt had been bought by a good client of Jimmy's, and that was nice, too. I didn't want to listen to any more. Not for a while, anyway, until some of the hurting had eased. Which I supposed it must do, eventually, though I couldn't imagine how.

We went somewhere for supper. I had a bowl of soup. I couldn't possibly have swallowed anything else.

"Are you all right, Stephany?" Cam asked gently.

"Sure. I'm fine," I said, trying to sound as though I meant it. But I couldn't force any kind of a smile to reassure her.

I was terribly tired, confused, and angry. I'd been able to deal well enough with this during the past several months because there'd been so much to do. Now, suddenly, there was nothing. I supposed, deep down somewhere, I'd expected something to happen to save our farm and our horses. Right up to the last minute, I hadn't been able to believe that everything would be gone.

Cam had found an apartment for us near the town, so we at least had a roof. It was nice to know that Rosie was safe at Jimmy's, even though strangers were caring for her, which wasn't the same at all. We'd even found a new home for Milton and Samantha at a nearby farm, so they'd be okay.

I struggled through the weary fog in my mind, trying to find something nice to think about. But it was hard.

Jimmy had offered me a job helping with his yearlings the next summer. Of course, I'd said yes, right away. Rosie would be there, too—at least I could ride her now and then. But it was all bits and pieces. Kind of like a scattering of corn, I decided, thrown into a pen for chickens. Scraps of busywork and nothing to tie it all together. The swing of the seasons wouldn't matter, the way they had at the farm. I missed Mom and Dad and all the horses in our care, and Thunder Rock, and the exciting expectations of foals to come, and those planned for the year after—there was no feeling of continuity that I could find anywhere.

"I've got to get back to Florida tomorrow," I heard Jimmy saying. "I've been lucky enough to have a good assistant there to keep an eye on things, but there are some big races coming up and I should be with the horses."

"You've done more than enough already," Cam said quietly. "We'll manage now, but you've been wonderful."

"There wasn't really all that much I could do," said Jimmy. "I couldn't stop what happened to you, much as I wished I could—" He took a deep breath. "But there is one thing. I want to tell you a story."

I knew he was trying to get through our sadness. I tried to pay attention and made an effort to look interested.

"Do you remember the Northern Dancer colt that was syndicated last fall for so many millions of dollars?"

Cam and I both nodded. Of course we remembered. The horse had won just about every big race in the country and had been considered too valuable to risk injury on the racetrack any longer. He'd been sold to a syndicate in Europe, where he was to go to stand at stud.

"The kind of horse that real dreams are made of," Cam said with a tired smile.

"But he was killed just a few weeks ago," I interrupted flatly. In the plane, flying over the Atlantic, the horse had suddenly panicked. Horses were always unpredictable, no matter what. There'd been a vet and several good attendants traveling with him, but nothing they'd done had helped. Finally, to save the lives of the plane crew and everyone else, before the colt kicked out the side of the plane and sent it crashing into the water below, the vet had been forced to destroy him.

I glanced up at Jimmy. What kind of story was this to tell us now—especially since we already knew what had happened to the splendid horse—after all the sadnesses we'd just been through ourselves?

"Such a terrible loss of a truly exceptional horse," Cam said. "Never to have had the chance to pass on his brilliance . . . I heard he had mares booked to him in France for at least the next five years. And now, no foals at all to carry on his line—"

"But that's exactly it, you see," said Jimmy. "There is one."

"Wow." Even I was impressed. "How marvelous. Who got so lucky?"

"Rosie did," said Jimmy.

"You're joking," I said, staring at the red and white tablecloth. "And that's not fair. Not right now, not after what we've been through—"

"I'm not joking," Jimmy said. I looked up at him again. He did look perfectly serious.

"I knew the farm manager where the colt was staying while the international agency waited for export papers," he said. "And I'm training two horses for one of the men who bought shares in the colt. So I heard about it when suddenly the insurance company or a nervous new owner wanted a test mare for their horse before they sent him on to Europe.

"The mares at the farm were all in foal or had already

been sent off to other stud farms. They were in a real pickle. I said I happened to have just the kind of mare they needed, but they couldn't have her unless they promised to sign all the right papers so the foal, if there was one, could be correctly registered."

"And so you took Rosie," I said, staring at him now without blinking. "That's why that crazy trip to pick her up in the middle of the night—"

"They wanted the mare right away," Jimmy said. "And I couldn't tell you what for. There was too big a chance for disappointment."

Too much. I felt as though I must look like a silly goldfish gaping in its bowl. I shut my mouth. The steamy clatter of the little restaurant went on around us, the waitress refilled coffee cups—

No wonder Jimmy had been in such a fuss over Rosie after the fire. He'd had extra reason to be, knowing what he did.

"She's definitely in foal," Jimmy said. "Dr. Bailey has signed the certificate. He gave a copy to me just this morning so I could give it to you tonight."

My mind soared with joy as it hadn't done for a long, long time. Rosie. She'd been like a shining silver thread weaving through our lives for so many years, and suddenly she was carrying a whole bundle of possible hopes for us—

Cam threw her head back and laughed with delight. "Our band of broodmares. Our string of racehorses. A whole new Thunder Rock, and all of them Rosie. . . . Jimmy, I don't know what I can say—"

"No one knows except those of us directly involved," Jimmy said cautiously. "After all, there's still a long time to wait for the foal. But, if everything goes well—"

"I can bear this kind of waiting," said Cam, reaching out to hug Jimmy.

I closed my eyes, half numb with shock. What would a foal like that be worth? And Rosie, keeping her own secrets—she wouldn't show she was in foal for several more months. What a dramatic reaction there would be in the breeding and racing world if a foal sired by that incredible young horse was safely born— More than the value of the prospective foal, though, it made everything different. I pictured Rosie with a foal of her very own, caring for it in her own wise and gentle way. Bloodlines of the absolute best in the entire world, carrying on into a future . . . .

Cam and Jimmy left the coffee shop hand in hand. I followed them into the soft Virginia night. It looked as though there was a new tomorrow out there, after all. It was sure beginning to look that way.

j   1
Doty, J.

If wishes were horses

4-26-85